PASSIONS RAGED HOT AS A PRAIRIE FIRE IN THE DAKOTA TOWN CALLED RED BUFFALO

Del Harrigan—His mission was saving souls, not killing—but some men are born for violence, not lives of peace.

Eagle Claw—Indian haters hanged one of his tribe, so this powerful Sioux chief is trading the peace pipe for settler's blood.

Ginny Wheeler—Her first husband broke her heart, but now the beautiful widow will find out just how good—and bad—a man can be.

Perry Prince—Money is his god and gambling his game, so the saloon owner wants his pound of flesh—and all of Ginny Wheeler.

Helen Coffman—Beauty is only skin deep in this scheming lady—she wants Del Harrigan either in her bed . . . or six feet under.

The Stagecoach Series
Ask your bookseller for the books you have missed

STAGECOACH STATION 41:
RED BUFFALO

Hank Mitchum

Created by the producers of
**Wagons West, The Badge,
Abilene,** and **Faraday.**

Book Creations Inc., Canaan, NY · Lyle Kenyon Engel, Founder

BANTAM BOOKS
TORONTO · NEW YORK · LONDON · SYDNEY · AUCKLAND

RED BUFFALO

*A Bantam Book / published by arrangement with
Book Creations, Inc.*

Bantam edition / May 1989

*Produced by Book Creations, Inc.
Lyle Kenyon Engel, Founder*

ISBN 0-553-27907-6

Published simultaneously in the United States and Canada

*Bantam Books are published by Bantam Books, a division of Bantam
Doubleday Dell Publishing Group, Inc. Its trademark, consisting of
the words "Bantam Books" and the portrayal of a rooster, is
Registered in U.S. Patent and Trademark Office and in other
countries. Marca Registrada. Bantam Books, 666 Fifth Avenue,
New York, New York 10103.*

PRINTED IN THE UNITED STATES OF AMERICA

0 9 8 7 6 5 4 3 2 1

STAGECOACH STATION 41:

RED BUFFALO

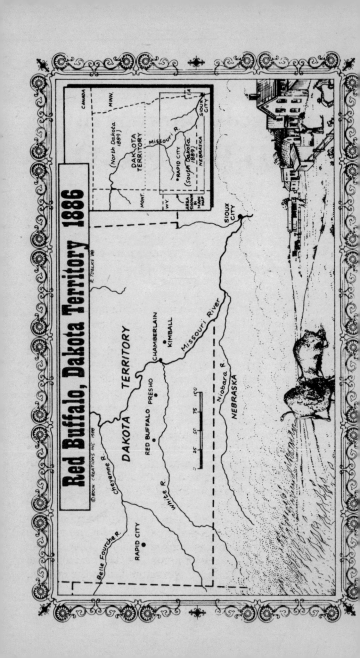

Chapter One

It was late morning when the huge locomotive chugged into the depot, then squealed and hissed to a halt, belching billows of black smoke and white steam that temporarily blocked out the sky. Throngs of people waited at the station platform, eagerly scanning the railroad cars for the sight of familiar faces.

The passengers alighted to meet friends and relatives—some with handshakes, some with embraces, and some with tears. Their reception was enhanced by the distant but distinct strains of a patriotic march being played by an unseen brass band, for the town of Sioux City, Iowa, was celebrating the nation's one hundredth birthday. The streets around the train station were bustling with people, and amid their cheers and shouts could be heard the occasional burst of firecrackers.

One of the last passengers to leave the train was a strikingly handsome man, extremely tall and muscular, in his late twenties. He was smartly dressed in a black pin-striped suit with matching vest, white shirt, string tie, and shiny black boots. A gold watch fob dangled from his vest, and he wore a light gray, broad-brimmed Stetson. Clutched in his left hand was a black valise bearing the monogram D. W. H., and as he stepped from the train, he set the valise on the platform and looked around. The rousing music, as well as the sight of numerous flags waving from rooftops and in the hands of spectators lining the streets, made him smile proudly.

He briefly removed his hat in the early July heat to mop his brow, and the sun glistened on his neatly trimmed black hair and thick mustache. Then, replacing the hat and stooping to pick up the valise, he strode across the platform and entered the railway office. Approaching the barred window, he said to the agent on duty, "My name is Delbert W. Harrigan, sir. I just came in on the eleven-fifteen. My trunk will be unloaded shortly, I assume, and I'd like to arrange that it be sent over to the Butterfield stagecoach office. I'll be taking the Rapid City stage tomorrow morning."

"Ah, so you'll be headin' into Dakota Territory, eh? Well, I'll be glad to do that for you, Mr. Harrigan," said the agent. "The trunk'll be there within the hour."

"Thanks. I appreciate it." Harrigan started to leave but then checked himself. "Oh, by the way, I made a reservation by wire for a room at the Riverview Hotel for tonight. How do I find it from here?"

The clerk gave him directions, concluding, "You can't miss it."

"Thanks again," Harrigan responded, and walked back outside into the late morning sun.

As he left the terminal, two young women were approaching it. Passing them, Del Harrigan overheard one of them comment to her friend, "How curious. That exceptionally good-looking fellow certainly has the bearing of a military man, but his clothes are all wrong. He's got to be a gambler. They always dress sharply like that."

Harrigan chuckled to himself, not at all surprised by the young woman's observation, for he had heard similar comments throughout his journey. Shaking his head bemusedly, he took a moment to get his bearings and then followed the railroad agent's directions, weaving his way among the crowd until he reached Main Street, which was packed with people, saddle horses, surreys, wagons, and buggies. His path took him close to the brass band he had been hearing since his arrival, and he stopped for a moment to listen and to look at the huge crowd gathered around it.

Proceeding along the street, Harrigan noted the variety of shops, stores, saloons, and offices on the way to the hotel, which was one block farther down. The railway agent had been right: the Riverview Hotel was huge and ornate and impossible to miss. It had the look of a southern mansion: broad, sweeping porch and elegant, towering white pillars. A massive sign indicated that the building housed not only the hotel but also the Silver Palace Saloon and Casino. Harrigan paused to gaze up at the magnificent facade, but then his attention was distracted by a small group nearby. The town marshal was sternly lecturing a group of teenage boys, explaining the danger of setting off firecrackers in town with so many people crowding the streets. With a final warning the marshal sent the boys, properly chastened, on their way.

The lawman turned to move on, and he saw Harrigan smiling sympathetically at him. Returning the smile, he walked up to him and said, "Howdy, stranger. Guess you heard me layin' the law down to those kids."

"I did indeed," Harrigan confirmed, nodding, "and I certainly hope your words will sink in."

Lifting his hat and scratching his head, the lawman mused, "I sure hope so—but I was a kid myself once, and I sort of doubt it." Dropping his hat back in place, he extended his right hand. "I'm Sid Cobb."

Gripping the marshal's hand solidly, Harrigan introduced himself.

"You here for the celebration?" the lawman asked.

"I'll enjoy it while I'm here, but actually I'm just passing through. I just came in on the train, and I'll be taking the Rapid City stage in the morning."

"You from Rapid City?"

"No, sir. I'm from Pennsylvania; Philadelphia, to be exact."

"Got business in Rapid City?"

"No, sir. Actually, I'm not going all the way to Rapid City. Just to Red Buffalo, which is about a hundred miles east of there."

Cobb rubbed his chin, looking down, and said, "Red

3

Buffalo . . . Red Buffalo. . . . Well, you got me, son. Don't know that I've ever heard of the place."

"Well, according to the Butterfield agent, it's three hundred miles northwest of here. The stage will be following the Missouri River for quite a distance, or at least that's my guess."

Looking him up and down, Cobb commented, "Then I take it you've never been there before. Are you plannin' on openin' up a new casino there or somethin'?"

Harrigan laughed. "No, nothing of the kind." Shifting his valise from one hand to the other, he smiled at the lawman and, gesturing toward the hotel, said, "Well, if you'll excuse me, I must register—and perhaps freshen up a bit. It's been a long while between hotel rooms."

"Oh, sorry! I didn't mean to hold you up." Cobb touched his hat brim and said, "Enjoy your stay. We've got us a nice town here."

"Thanks, Marshal."

Harrigan mounted the broad stairway and entered the hotel. Striding across the spacious, well-appointed lobby to the registry desk, he noticed that off to the left was the entrance to the hotel restaurant as well as to the gaming room. He was pleased that the hotel had its own dining facilities, which would save him the trouble of having to locate a restaurant later on that evening.

At the desk, Del Harrigan was greeted by the young, bookish clerk. "Welcome to the Riverview, sir," the man declared, looking up and smiling amiably through his pince-nez glasses. "How may I help you?"

"I have a reservation for tonight," the dark-haired man replied. "Name's Harrigan, D. W. Harrigan."

"Ah, yes, sir. We have you in room eleven, which is at the top of the stairs and to the left," the clerk informed him. "I hope that it meets with your approval. It has quite a good view of the Missouri River—which, of course, is where the hotel got its name." Spinning the register around for Harrigan to sign, the clerk indicated the pen and inkwell.

"I'm sure that will do nicely, thanks."

4

While Harrigan scratched his signature on the register, the clerk took a key from one of the pigeonholes behind him and laid it on the desk. He read the entry and commented, "I see that you're from Philadelphia. Is the Centennial Exposition as wonderful as it sounds from all the newspaper accounts I've read?"

Smiling and nodding, Harrigan assured the clerk, "It certainly is. One of the marvels on display is a section of that statue the French nation is giving to America to celebrate our independence. I tell you, it'll be a virtual colossus when it's completed. All that's exhibited at the Centennial is the hand, but you can actually climb up the arm, through the hand, and stand on the torch!"

"My goodness!" the clerk exclaimed. "What other marvels do they have?"

"They have things on display there that are absolutely unique. Why, the machines alone take up thousands of square feet. Of course, I must say that some of the inventions are virtually useless—and everyone else seemed to agree with me."

"Oh, really? What types of inventions?"

Chuckling, Harrigan told him, "For example, a professor—I believe his name is Bell—has created a gadget he calls a telephone. However, it fails to do anything but carry the human voice, so there's obviously not much use for it."

The clerk laughed. "The very idea! Why in the world would anyone need a device like that? Ah, well. I suppose all manner of things get invented every year that aren't good for anything." He grew serious then and asked, "Tell me, has the news of the awful massacre in Montana reached the East Coast yet?"

"I assume you're talking about Custer at the Little Big Horn a week and a half ago?"

"Yes, sir."

"The news had just hit Philadelphia when I left."

Shaking his head sadly, the clerk commented, "I daresay that General Custer and his men will go down in history as heroes. And rightly they should. What an incredible act of bravery—a small handful of men going up against thousands of Sioux. They died fighting like true soldiers, that's for sure."

Harrigan's mouth became an angry thin line, and he told the clerk crustily, "The *men* of the Seventh Cavalry truly are heroes, but George Armstrong Custer was a glory boy."

Blinking in surprise, the clerk asked, "What do you mean, sir?"

"Custer's men were needlessly slaughtered at the Little Big Horn because he disobeyed his commander's orders when he attacked the Sioux camp. Although he had no idea how many Indians were encamped along the river, he figured by wiping them out, he'd find himself a spot in the history books. I feel sorrow for his men—after all, they had no choice but to obey their commanding officer's orders—but as far as I'm concerned, Custer was no hero." Harrigan paused a few moments and then added, "And by the way, just to set the record straight, Custer wasn't a general. He was a colonel."

Nonplussed, the clerk gasped, "But sir, I've heard him called General Custer ever since I was a child!"

"He was a brevet general in the Civil War, and when the war ended, he became a colonel again. But he much preferred being known as general, so he still called himself that. As I said, he was a glory boy."

Dumbfounded to hear such words, the clerk stared at him and queried, "Are you in the military, Mr. Harrigan?"

"I used to be," Harrigan replied tersely, picking up his valise. As he mounted the stairs, he glanced back over his shoulder to see the clerk still staring after him.

Entering room number eleven, Harrigan placed the valise on the bed and looked around, then opened the windows. He started to remove his jacket, thinking briefly about taking either a nap or a bath, but then he slipped it back on and headed for the door. Realizing that he had the whole afternoon before him, he decided he might as well join in the centennial celebration.

As Harrigan stepped out of the hotel, he saw a parade

coming down the street. It was led by several horsemen riding abreast, their saddles gaily decorated with red, white, and blue ribbons, the middle rider holding up a large American flag on a long pole.

At the sight of the oncoming riders, people immediately cleared the road and lined the boardwalks on both sides of the street. Children pushed their way to the edges of the boardwalk, squeezing between columns of legs to get a better view.

Behind the riders marched a brass band made up of over twenty men, all dressed in white uniforms and tall white hats striped with red and blue. The flag waving in the breeze seemed to be keeping time to the snappy march, a big bass drum booming out the beat. The band was followed by more riders as well as wagons made up as floats, all bedecked with flags, flowers, banners, and ribbons of red, white, and blue.

The long line of riders and floats went on for ten minutes, but the end of the parade was finally in sight. Just as the last marcher strode by and the crowd began filtering back into the street, the teenage boys admonished earlier by the marshal lit a string of firecrackers and threw them under a wagon parked up the street.

When the firecrackers exploded, they sounded like a firing Gatling gun, and the two draft horses yoked to the wagon bolted. A woman crossing the street screamed and pointed at the charging wild-eyed team with its bounding wagon behind it. Everyone immediately scattered for the boardwalks. A young mother dragged her two small children from the middle of the street toward the safety of the boardwalk, and they had barely reached it when her little girl, not understanding the impending danger, jerked free of her mother and backed directly into the path of the galloping team.

Frozen with fear and clutching her other child, the mother screamed in horror as the wagon bore down on the girl. When Harrigan turned to see what the cries were about, he reacted instantly, dashed into the street, and seized the child. Realizing that he would not have enough time to get out of the way, he quickly gauged the space between the two horses as well as the wagon wheels, and then he pushed the child to the ground. He leaped on top of her, covering her fragile body with his, and positioned himself between the pairs of thundering hooves and the spinning wheels. Closing his eyes, he prayed that his judgment was accurate and that the team and wagon would pass harmlessly over them.

As the dust settled, Harrigan breathed an enormous sigh of relief and stood up, lifting the whimpering child into his arms. The onlookers all seemed to have been holding their breath as well, and now, seeing that the stranger's heroic deed had been successful, they abruptly found their voices again. Gathering around, they closed in tight as Harrigan carried the little girl over to her weeping mother.

It was no easy task to get the child to loosen her grip around Harrigan's neck, but at the sight of her mother, she finally let go. "There you are, little one," the tall man told her, smiling gently. "You're safe and sound."

The young mother broke into sobs. Handing her other child to a friend, she gathered her daughter in her arms, clutching her tightly. Looking up at Harrigan, she exclaimed, "Oh, bless you, sir! I'll be eternally beholden to you!"

Harrigan's handsome face flushed. "There's no need to be, ma'am," he assured her humbly. "I just happened to be in the right place at the right time."

Shaking her head, the mother said, "There were lots of other men on the street, sir, but you were the only one willing to risk your life to save my Annie." With that, she raised up on her toes and kissed his smudged cheek.

A rousing cheer erupted among the crowd. Harrigan touched the spot where the woman had kissed him, grinned boyishly at her, and then turned and walked away. As he headed for the hotel, dusting himself off, he saw the horses and wagon that had so nearly figured in tragedy being led back along the street. Miraculously, the horses had quickly run themselves out around the town square and had been easily approached. Looking at the docile pair of drays, Harrigan found it hard to believe that they were the same horses that had been so wild just minutes before. Shaking his head, he started mounting the stairs to the hotel. He was halfway up when a teenage boy came running after him with a light gray Stetson in his right hand.

"You forgot your hat, mister!" cried the boy, bounding up the stairs.

Harrigan grinned and reached for the hat. "Thanks, son. In all that excitement, I hadn't missed it—but I'd have been looking for it pretty soon." Then he looked sharply at the youth. "I hope you weren't one of the kids whose mischief made those horses spook."

The boy shook his head vehemently. "No, sir, I wasn't." He looked around, as if to make sure no one could overhear him, and then continued, "But I do know who they were—and I'm pretty sure they'll never do anything like that again. Not after what happened."

"Well, I'm glad to hear it. And thanks for bringing me my hat."

The boy turned and darted down the steps. Del Harrigan watched him go as he slapped the hat against his leg, freeing it of the dust. He punched it back into shape as he mounted the rest of the steps and entered the hotel. Once inside, he slipped as unobtrusively as possible up the stairs to his room. He had had enough fuss made over him for one day, and he was going to do his darnedest to avoid any more.

Chapter Two

A warm breeze was blowing in through the two open windows, fluttering the curtains, when Del Harrigan stepped into his room. Laying his hat on the dresser, he stripped off his jacket and trousers and draped them carefully on the bed. He walked over to the washstand, dipped a cloth into the washbowl, and wrung it out. Then he began brushing the damp cloth over his dirt-smeared clothes. After working on the garments for several minutes, until they were reasonably clean, he hung them up to dry and then wearily stretched his long frame out on the bed.

Sweat began trickling down his face and body; the blazing afternoon sun had turned the small hotel room into an oven. He considered taking out another suit of clothes and getting dressed again to escape the closeness of his quarters, but he was tired from both the long train ride and the unexpected incident in the street, and he needed to rest for a while. He told himself that if he just lay still with his eyes closed, soon he would not feel the heat.

The steady hum of noise filtering up from the street and the enveloping heat made Del Harrigan extremely torpid, and he drifted off, floating back through time and space. Suddenly he was in an open field rimmed by forest, surrounded by booming cannon and barking rifles. Bullets chewed into the ground near his feet and shells exploded nearby, making his ears ring. Revolver in hand, firing periodically over his shoulder, he was dashing across the field in an attempt to reach the protection of the trees. There were dead men all around him, sprawled on the grass. Some wore blue; others wore gray. A few yards to his left, a man in blue lying in a pool of his own blood reached his hand desperately toward Harrigan, calling, "Captain! Captain! Help me!"

Holstering his revolver, Harrigan rushed to the man's side, knelt down, and lifted him up. With bullets whining and artillery shells exploding all around him, he carried the wounded Union soldier into the sheltering forest. He was trying to find a place to lay him down when suddenly two men in gray came at him, bayonets fixed on their long-barreled rifles. When he turned toward them, one of the Confederates stabbed with his bayonet, driving it deep into the wounded man's chest.

Captain Delbert Harrigan had no choice. Dropping the now-dead soldier, he dodged the thrust of the second man, drew his revolver, and fired . . . but the hammer slammed down on a spent shell. He had not bothered to count his shots as he ran across the open field, and his gun was empty.

Dropping the useless weapon to the ground, Harrigan readied himself. The first Rebel was busy pulling his bayonet out of the dead Union soldier; the second let out a high-pitched yell and charged. Harrigan sidestepped in time and the man in gray ran past him. The tip of his bayonet struck a tree and lodged itself deep in the wood.

The Rebel, who had now lost the use of his rifle and bayonet, wheeled about, but Harrigan struck with the flat of his hand on the man's windpipe. He went down, gagging and choking, and Harrigan finished him off with a fierce blow to the back of the neck.

Pivoting about, he saw the other Rebel coming at him, bayonet pointed straight for his chest. Harrigan feinted a jump to his left, but then he leaped to the right. The ploy threw the Rebel off, and he stumbled past. Harrigan reached down and scooped up his revolver just as the man whirled around. When the Rebel charged again, the captain threw the gun, hitting the man on the forehead. The force of the blow staggered the soldier, and Harrigan jerked the rifle from his hands. Before the man could right himself, the bayonet was plunged into his throat. He slumped to the ground, dead, the point of the blade sticking out the back of his neck.

With the roar of guns and exploding shells thundering in his ears, Harrigan quickly looked around and then dashed through the trees. The fighting had separated him from his unit, and he had to find them. . . .

Abruptly Del Harrigan was back in his room at the Riverview Hotel. Blinking his eyes, he took a moment or two to get his bearings. The sun had gone down, and twilight had settled. The noise in the streets had subsided, and now there was only the soft sound of a few voices and the occasional clip-clopping of a solitary horse.

The effects of the dream lingered as he rose from the bed and washed his face at the washstand. He had relived many of his Civil War battles in true-to-life dreams, but the most vivid ones—and the ones that came back the most often—were those battles in which he had killed enemy soldiers with his bare hands. There was something haunting about actually touching the enemy and taking his life without a weapon. He shuddered and splashed cold water on his face.

Lighting the ceiling lamp, Harrigan dressed hurriedly and then left the room. When he reached the bottom of the stairs, he strode across the lobby and into the dining room, which, as he discovered, shared an enormous space with the saloon and casino. The bar and gaming area were situated a few steps below the dining tables. An elegantly dressed, middle-aged hostess guided Harrigan to a table, telling him that a waiter would be with him shortly.

Sitting down at the table, Harrigan let his eyes roam around the room. The first things he noticed were fancy crystal chandeliers hanging from the high, ornate ceiling. They were alive with burning wicks and cast a warm glow over everything. From where he sat, he had a full view of the plush casino, the long rounded bar, and the small stage at the back of the saloon, directly opposite the

12

dining room. There was an upright piano next to the stage, and a small skinny man wearing a flat-topped straw hat and bright red arm garters was playing a melodic ballad. A large, buxom woman with heavy powder and paint on her face was singing from the stage—though no one seemed to be listening.

The crowd was in a jovial and boisterous mood, and the celebration that had been going on since early morning seemed—at least in this place—to have abated little. The cavernous room was draped with tricolored bunting and numerous American flags; one huge flag was hanging on the back wall behind the stage.

The waiter came and took his order. A few minutes later, an elegantly suited man approached Harrigan's table. Smiling, he said, "Pardon me for intruding upon you, Mr. Harrigan. My name is Raymond Welch, and I am the manager of this establishment. I saw with my own eyes your heroism in saving that young child from a horrible death, and, to express some small appreciation for what you've done, I would be honored if you'd allow me to offer your meal at no charge."

Smiling up at Welch, Harrigan assured him, "I only helped out where I was needed, sir, and you don't owe me anything. I fully expect to pay for my meal."

"Oh, but that would rob me of so much pleasure, my good fellow," countered Welch.

Harrigan shrugged his broad shoulders. "Well . . . since you put it that way . . . all right. By the way, how did you know my name?"

The manager smiled. "From the hotel clerk, sir— although I'm sure everybody in town knows your name by now."

Harrigan shook his head, embarrassed by his sudden fame. He thanked Welch, and the manager bowed slightly, moving off when the food arrived.

The man from Philadelphia had just started his meal when he heard a commotion behind him. He turned to see four big, rough-looking men wearing dirty old Confederate uniforms shove their way past the astonished hostess and enter the dining hall. When they strode by his table, heading for the saloon area, Harrigan noticed that their campaign hats were black from sweat, and he could smell the foul odor of their bodies. The biggest man, who was apparently the leader, carried a thick piece of folded cloth in one of his meaty hands.

The bearded, long-haired men pushed their way to the center of the saloon, rudely shoving other patrons out of the way. Then they made their way over to the stage, and while three of the men positioned themselves in front of it, the leader mounted the steps and looked defiantly out at the audience. The heavyset woman who had been warbling popular tunes looked at the man aghast, and in a huff she hurried from the stage. Realizing that he was no longer accompanying her, the piano player turned his head, saw what was going on, and stopped playing.

The Rebel stood glaring out at the patrons for a long moment and then bawled loudly, "Hey, listen up!"

The noise level in the saloon lowered somewhat, but a number of people continued to talk. Angered, the Rebel leader whipped out his revolver and fired it into the ceiling. The roar of the gun brought immediate silence as the cloud of blue-white gun smoke rose toward the bright chandeliers, and the acrid smell of burnt powder filled the air.

With the unmistakable accent of a southerner, the massive man bellowed, "My name is Cap'n Hubert Driggers of the Confederate Army, and these fine gentlemen with me are my lieutenants. When we rode into this here town late this afternoon and saw all these Union flags everywhere . . . well, we took a mighty great offense at that. Though you stinkin' Yankees may have won the war, to rectify matters, me and my men, we're gonna give all you folks the chance to honor the true flag of our nation, the flag of the Confederacy."

Angry words rose from the crowd, and almost in unison, many of the men surged forward toward the stage. But at a signal from Driggers, his three cohorts whipped out their revolvers and pointed them at the crowd, effectively staying everyone's movement.

"Like I said," Driggers growled, "you're gonna honor the true flag—and your reverence had better be to my satisfaction."

With a flourish, he unfurled the cloth in his hands to reveal a large Confederate flag. Then he turned to the huge American flag draped on the wall behind him and unceremoniously ripped it down, quickly hanging the Rebel flag in its place.

A well-built young man standing at the bar apparently had had enough. Ignoring the threatening revolvers, he stormed his way to the stage and confronted Driggers, shouting, "I'd say you're one good reason why the nation's lucky the South lost the war, mister. Now, you and your fellow polecats drag your carcasses out of here, or we'll throw you out!"

Driggers stared balefully at the young man. "So you want to challenge me, do you, friend?" the Rebel fumed, his voice sounding as raspy as a coarse file. He grunted to one of his men, "Billy Bob, show this fella how we deal with disobedience in the Confederate Army."

The "lieutenant" stepped up beside the man and savagely hit him on the head with the revolver, crushing the young man to the floor. The other Rebels waved their muzzles back and forth to ward off any retaliation from other men in the saloon.

With a defiant look in his blazing eyes, Driggers yelled, "Anybody else want to speak his piece?"

Silence prevailed.

Del Harrigan looked on from his table, infuriated. He itched to teach these men a lesson, but he held back, knowing somebody would probably get killed if he interfered. Gripping the edge of the table, he forced himself to stay put, telling himself that no doubt the southerners would have their say for a while and then be gone. With luck, everyone else would realize the same thing and would also stay calm, and the only person to be hurt would be the man who now lay on the floor, moaning softly.

The patrons looked at each other, apparently waiting to see what the others would do. Harrigan heard someone behind him suggest quietly that the marshal be summoned and a man slipped out, apparently to do so, but no one seemed willing to do anything that would risk further angering the Rebels.

Then Captain Hubert Driggers went too far. He suddenly began stomping on Old Glory, and a collective gasp rose from the patrons. That was all Del Harrigan could take. Seeing the flag he loved trampled by a loudmouthed Rebel bully lit a fuse inside the former Union officer, and he found himself charging across the large room straight for Hubert Driggers.

When the three "lieutenants" saw the big man coming their way, one of them bellowed, "Hey, you! Whaddya think you're doin'?"

"I'm calling a halt to these proceedings!" Harrigan commanded. "Captain, I insist that you and your men leave at once!"

Driggers turned to confront the new aggressor, but he was too late. Harrigan leaped onto the stage and hurled himself forward just as Driggers lifted his revolver. The two men slammed against the rear wall, and the revolver slipped from Driggers's hand, clattering to the floor.

Harrigan regained his balance first and backed away two steps, waiting for the other man to get to his feet. While Driggers clawed his way up the wall, Harrigan shouted, "Nobody tramples on that flag in my presence, mister! Now, pick it up off the floor and hang it back where it belongs!"

Straightening his back and looking down at his somewhat shorter challenger, Driggers spat, "Make me, Yankee!"

Harrigan glared at the man and retorted, "It will be my pleasure!"

Hubert Driggers's three cohorts hurried onto the stage to assist their captain. But looking past Harrigan, Driggers told them, "Leave us alone, men. I'll handle this here

16

pretty boy all by myself. I'm gonna make him eat that flag inch by inch—without any salt or pepper."

As Driggers dropped into a crouch, Del Harrigan made his move. He threw a hard right at the man's bearded jaw and slammed him against the wall. Then he caught him with a powerful left hook as Driggers bounded off the wall, and the blow whipped the Rebel's head sideways.

Driggers righted himself and lashed out with a meaty fist at his opponent, but his knuckles only grazed Harrigan's left cheek and did no damage. He swung again and missed, and in return took a savage blow that split his lips and bloodied his mouth. Harrigan grabbed him by the shirt and pummeled him again, and Driggers sailed backward across the stage. As he lay there trying to clear his head, Harrigan towered over him and demanded, "Pick up the flag. Now!"

"Pick it up yourself, Yankee," the Rebel sneered as he slowly brought himself erect and then with great deliberation spat on the Stars and Stripes. Infuriated, Harrigan lunged at him. Driggers raised his arms to defend himself, but he stood no chance against the fists beating mercilessly against his face.

He was soon on the floor again. Abruptly, his cohort Billy Bob decided it was time to rescue his friend, and he leaped onto the stage and came after Harrigan, using his pistol like a club.

Harrigan waited until the Rebel swung the weapon and, carefully dodging the blow, seized the man's wrist and twisted it violently. The man howled as the gun dropped from his hand and clattered to the floor. Reaching over, Harrigan sharply wrenched the man's arm up behind his back, snapping it, and Billy Bob fell to his knees, screaming with pain.

The two other Rebels were spurred into action and sprang to the aid of their cohorts, but it was too late. The male patrons in the saloon, stirred by Del Harrigan's courage, suddenly swarmed after the two men, disarming them and pinning them to the floor.

Del Harrigan made his way to the back of the stage, where Hubert Driggers was now on one knee, attempting to stand. Breathing hard, Harrigan stood over him and panted, "Are you ready to pick up the flag?"

Blood was running from Driggers's split lips and a crimson stream trickled from his left nostril. His eyes were puffy, his face swollen and discolored. His mouth sagged as he sucked hard for air, but he made no response.

The man from Philadelphia hissed, "I asked you a question, Driggers. Are you ready to pick up the flag?"

Rising slowly to his feet, Driggers turned his wrecked face toward Harrigan. "Yes, suh," he answered quietly. He staggered to where the American flag lay on the floor and picked it up. Folding it carefully, he extended it to his conqueror.

Shaking his head, Harrigan said flatly, "That isn't good enough. You turn your carcass around and pull that Confederate rag off the wall. I want Old Glory right back where she was."

While Driggers was obeying his command, Harrigan bent down and picked up the Rebel leader's revolver. Then he picked up Billy Bob's gun as well. Breaking open both weapons, he spilled the cartridges on the floor. He looked over to the patrons who held the other two Rebels and ordered, "Empty their guns, gentlemen . . . and keep yours trained on them." While his order was being followed, he jammed the empty gun back in Billy Bob's holster, then grabbed him by the shirt collar and lifted him to his feet, ignoring his cries of pain.

When Driggers had rehung the Stars and Stripes, Harrigan nodded and told him disdainfully, "Well done, Captain Driggers. You must have been very good at obeying your superior officers." Handing Billy Bob over, he went on, "Now, I'll give you one last order before you leave, and that's to take your friend to get his shoulder reset. Maybe if you ask nicely, somebody here will tell you where to find a doctor. Then I'd suggest you and your men get out of this town."

The two Rebels hobbled down off the stage and joined

their cohorts just as Marshal Cobb rushed in. Making his way to the stage, the lawman looked up at Del Harrigan and said with a smile, "I've just been told what's been going on here, Mr. Harrigan. You seem to be a one-man rescue team here in Sioux City, don't you?" Turning, he looked the Rebels over and remarked, "Guess I need to lock these characters up for a few days and teach them a lesson."

"They've already had their lesson, Marshal," spoke up one of the patrons. "Mr. Harrigan here is a master teacher—as I'm sure that one with the injured arm will tell you. Besides, if you lock them up, they may infest the jail with their vermin."

Cobb nodded. "Okay. Well, in that case go ahead and tell them where to find Doc Wilson." He eyed Driggers sternly and told him, "As soon as your pal's been patched up, I want you men out of this town—and don't ever show your faces here again."

When the beaten Rebels had gone, someone in the crowd suggested they now had even more of a reason to celebrate.

Marshal Cobb nodded his agreement. "Mr. Harrigan, I appreciate your handling those troublemakers. As I understand it, they might have killed somebody if you hadn't stepped in."

The tall man ran his fingers through his hair, looking slightly embarrassed by all the praise. "I must confess that I took action as much for myself as anything. You see, I went through four years of bloody battles during the war so Old Glory could fly freely in this country, and I wasn't about to let some diehard Confederates or anybody else throw my flag down and trample it. It was more than I could stomach."

"As it would be for me, as well," a voice interrupted.

Harrigan looked toward the speaker and watched as a man of about forty, wearing an expensive white linen suit, approached. Slender and of medium height, he wore his black hair parted in the middle and greased down flat. The dark-eyed man's most striking feature was a highly waxed handlebar mustache, the ends of which were elaborately curled.

Extending his soft, almost delicate hand, the man said, "Mr. Harrigan, I've been hearing about you all day. My name is Perry Prince, and I own this establishment. My manager has already informed me that he has offered you your meal at no charge. I feel that that is far too insufficient for all the help you have provided, so I would like to add that there will be no charge for your hotel room, and your drinks are on the house. I've instructed the bartender to give you whatever and as much as you want—be it whiskey or champagne."

"That's most generous of you, and I appreciate your offer, Mr. Prince," Harrigan responded, "but I feel it's only right that I pay for my hotel room. And as for the drinks, well, I'm really not interested. All I want to do is go back to my table and finish my meal."

Prince smiled sympathetically. "Only by now it's gone quite cold. But we'll order it up again for you—and I do insist that you accept your room without charge as well as your dinner."

Throwing up his hands in mock surrender, Harrigan laughed. "Very well, Mr. Prince, I give in."

"Good. We are all beholden to you, sir, and I'm only too pleased to be able to thank you in this small way."

It was almost an hour later when Del Harrigan finished his meal. Feeling the need for some fresh air, he left the hotel restaurant to take a brief walk before returning to his room for the evening. It had finally cooled off with the coming of night, and as Harrigan moved slowly along the streetlamp-lined street, relishing the change of temperature, he was unaware that hate-filled eyes were watching him from the shadows across the way.

When Harrigan reached the end of the block, four bulky shapes suddenly materialized out of the darkness of the cross street and stood in front of him, blocking his way. He stopped, staring intently at them—and in particular at Hubert Driggers's battered visage.

The man's face was contorted with hatred as he growled, "Too bad you didn't take our guns away from us, Yankee. They're reloaded now—and it's time for you to die."

Del Harrigan's body tensed as the Rebel captain, his hand splayed over the butt of his revolver, drawled wickedly, "I sure do hope you took a long look at the sunrise this mornin', Yankee pretty boy, 'cause it was the last one you'll ever see." Driggers paused a few seconds and then continued, "Now, mind you, ol' Hubie isn't gonna cut you down in cold blood. A southern gentleman wouldn't do a nasty thing like that. What's gonna happen is, you're gonna draw against me."

Holding the Rebel's gaze with his own, Harrigan said evenly, "I'm not wearing a gun."

Driggers grinned crookedly. "Come on now, mister. Everybody in these parts wears a gun."

Harrigan slowly opened his jacket to show the big Rebel that he was unarmed. He was still holding it open when Marshal Cobb, apparently summoned by a bystander who had witnessed the encounter, came racing onto the scene.

"Hold it right there!" the lawman shouted, pushing himself between Harrigan and Driggers. "In the name of the law, mister, I'm telling you to take your cronies and ride out of here right now, or you're gonna be mighty sorry."

Without a word, Driggers whipped out his gun and fired point-blank at the marshal. The slug ripped into Cobb's right shoulder, and the impact drove him backward into Harrigan. The two of them went down, the marshal landing virtually in Harrigan's lap. Reacting instantly, Harrigan snatched Cobb's revolver from its holster and fired at Driggers, hitting him in the rib cage.

Driggers slipped to the ground, still clutching his gun. Holding the wounded lawman in the crook of his left arm, Harrigan thumbed back the hammer of the revolver in his right hand and warned the Confederate captain, "Drop the gun, Driggers, or you're a dead man."

21

Gritting his teeth, the huge man ignored the warning. The intent to kill was clearly visible in his eyes as he brought the muzzle up.

Harrigan lined his gun on Driggers's forehead and squeezed the trigger. The gun bucked in his hand and Driggers flopped on his back, a small black hole in the middle of his forehead.

The other Rebels just stood there for a long moment, their trousers spattered with blood. Then one of them suddenly swore and drew his gun, but Harrigan fired instantly, drilling the man through the heart. As the echo of the report rattled among the clapboard buildings, Harrigan stared icily at the other two men and, his gun trained first on one and then the other, snapped, "Who's next?"

The two looked at each other and then back at Harrigan. "We . . . we ain't gonna do nothin', mister!" choked one of them.

"Throw your guns down!" ordered Harrigan.

Cautiously pulling their revolvers from their holsters, the two men dropped them as though they had suddenly turned red-hot.

Without taking his eyes off the Rebels, Harrigan eased the bleeding marshal to a comfortable position on the ground. Then he stood up and looked toward the crowd that had gathered at a safe distance. "Get a doctor!" he shouted, and two men hurried away.

Harrigan held the gun steady on the surviving Rebels and told them stonily, "You two pick up your buddies and get out of Sioux City immediately. I don't see any reason why the good people of this town should have to pay for burying the likes of you. But if you even think about looking back, they'll have to—since there won't be anyone left to haul *your* bodies off. Now, move!"

Working as fast as they could, the men picked up the bodies of their friends and carried them to their horses. They draped them over the saddles without bothering to tie them down and rode away into the night.

"Clear the way please! Clear the way!" an authoritative voice called. The doctor appeared and bent down to check the wounded marshal. After a brief examination, he looked up and reported, "Well, fortunately for Sid, he's in no serious danger. But I have to get that slug out as quickly as possible." The physician designated three men to carry the marshal to the clinic.

As the three men hoisted Cobb up, he looked at Harrigan through pain-clouded eyes and mumbled, "I'm sure glad . . . you're on . . . our side."

Harrigan watched as doctor and patient slowly made their way down the street. A man in the crowd stepped up and watched with him for a moment and then declared, "In all my life, I have never seen a man who could think so fast and act so quickly as you, Mr. Harrigan."

"I second that," another man offered. "And you're so good with a gun, besides. You wouldn't be some kind of lawman, would you, sir?"

"No," Harrigan replied, turning to head back toward the hotel, "I just had a lot of experience with weapons during the war. And I must say," he added, shaking his head with regret, "I did enough killing then to last a dozen lifetimes. I had hoped I would never have to kill again—but unfortunately those men just didn't give me a choice."

Chapter Three

Brilliant sunbeams filtered through the branches of the tall oaks and cottonwoods that lined the streets of Sioux City, Iowa. Del Harrigan had slept later than he had intended, and he had to gulp down his breakfast at the hotel restaurant in order to catch the Rapid City stagecoach in time. Picking up his black valise, he hurried outside, and as he made his way to the stage depot, he watched the cleaning up of the clutter left behind by the previous day's celebration.

That thought made him think of his suit, and he looked down at his jacket. He was pleased at how well the night clerk had had it cleaned and pressed, for it had taken quite a beating the night before. He felt quite dapper now, and as he drew near the Butterfield Overland Mail office, he tipped his hat and smiled flirtatiously at two young ladies walking by. Both women turned and giggled coyly, batting their eyes at him.

Harrigan felt elated and expansive. He rounded the corner of the depot and saw a six-horse team hitched to the waiting stagecoach, and the horses seemed to be echoing his mood as they bobbed their heads and snorted, their manes waving in the sunlight. The driver, shotgunner, and station agent were all busy loading luggage and freight parcels into the rear boot and overhead on the luggage rack, and Del Harrigan was pleased to see that his trunk was already lashed up top.

Three people stood on the boardwalk beside the coach,

watching with obvious interest, and Harrigan assumed they were his fellow passengers. Two of them, a man and woman in their midtwenties, were apparently husband and wife. The third person was an elderly man who Harrigan guessed would be well into his seventies. As he stepped beside them, the young woman plucked on her husband's sleeve and told him, "Albert, it seems that we'll have the pleasure of Mr. Harrigan's company on our journey." She smiled warmly yet shyly at the late arrival.

Harrigan doffed his hat and smiled in return. "Pardon me, ma'am, but you have an advantage over me. You know who I am, but I don't know your names."

The young man extended his hand. "Forgive us our rudeness, sir. My name is Albert Bittner, and this is my wife, Linna. We saw what you did at the Silver Palace last night."

Harrigan murmured polite greetings and then replaced his Stetson. Turning to the elderly man, he inquired, "And who might you be, sir?"

"My name's Will Stubbs. And although I didn't get to see the exhibition you put on last night, I certainly heard all about it at my hotel this morning." He paused a moment, adding, "Sorry, I didn't quite catch your name. Did Mr. Bittner say it's Harrison?"

"No, sir. Harrigan. Del Harrigan." Looking at each of the passengers in turn, he inquired, "How far are you traveling?"

Albert Bittner answered, "We're going all the way to Rapid City." Looking down at the older man, Bittner asked, "And where did you say you were heading, Mr. Stubbs?"

"Chamberlain. It's about halfway between here and Rapid City. I'm going out to live with my daughter and son-in-law." Throwing a glance at the coach, he commented wryly, "It's not exactly going to be like riding a train, is it? I've got a feeling we'll be looking forward to every single rest we take along the way. They tell me they stop every ten or fifteen miles to change horses—but I've got a sneaking suspicion they time it so that just when the passengers decide they've had their fill of bouncing and jostling and are thinking about getting out and walking the rest of the way, they're given a few minutes of relief. Then they forget how dreadful the ride was for just long enough. . . ."

His fellow passengers all laughed.

"Okay, folks," called the driver from up on the box. "You can go ahead and board. You're the only passengers riding with us right now, so take your pick of seating. We'll probably be picking up some others along the way, but you can stretch out in the meantime."

Del Harrigan stepped to the coach and opened the door for the other passengers, motioning for Linna Bittner to enter first. Albert took her hand and helped her in and then followed and sat down beside her. Will Stubbs climbed in across from them, and Del Harrigan slipped in beside him, closing the door. The agent waved to them from the boardwalk and called, "Hope you have a pleasant trip, folks!"

The stage was about to pull out when a stocky man in his early thirties, his face sweating from exertion, came running up out of breath and yelled, "Hold it, driver!" Turning to the agent, he asked, "Is there room for one more?"

"Sure thing." The agent told the driver to wait, and the two men went into the office. The new passenger dashed back outside in less than a minute, waving his ticket at the driver.

"Do you have any luggage?" the driver asked.

"Nope," the stocky man replied, still panting slightly. Opening the door, he climbed in and sat next to Harrigan, and the stage was already in motion before the man could close the door. With some effort, he pulled it shut and then reached into his pocket for a large white handkerchief and began mopping his glistening face. After attempting to smooth the wrinkles on his light tan suit and straighten his wildly askew tie, he smiled tentatively at the other passengers.

"Whew!" he sighed. "Just about missed it!" Running

26

the cloth along the back of his neck and then going over his face again, he told them, "I'm Mack Wheeler. I'm on my way to Red Buffalo." With that, he twisted in his seat and craned his neck to look out the window.

"That's where I'm going," spoke up Harrigan.

Wheeler's head came around, and he looked blankly at Harrigan. "Did you say something?"

"Yes, I said that I'm also heading for Red Buffalo."

"Oh, really? What a coincidence."

"Is Red Buffalo your home?" Harrigan asked politely.

Wheeler looked at him for a moment and then responded, "It used to be. I'm returning to visit, um, relatives." Mopping his still dripping face, the stocky man smiled weakly. Then, his hands shaking, he twisted around in the seat and stuck his head out the window again, looking back nervously through the dust cloud being churned up by the wheels, as if worried that someone was following the coach.

The four other passengers gave each other curious glances, and when Wheeler finally pulled his head in and squared around in the seat, Harrigan asked, "Expecting someone?"

There was fear in the man's eyes, but he tried to hide it as he said, "What?"

"Were you expecting someone to follow us?"

"Oh, uh . . . no. I . . . uh . . . it's just that I don't know if I'll ever see Sioux City again, and it holds some sentimental memories for me. I just wanted to take one last look."

The coach fell silent, as though all the passengers were suddenly reminded of their own destinations and destinies. Albert Bittner finally broke the silence when he looked admiringly at Del Harrigan and asked, "Tell us, sir, where did you learn to fight the way you did last night?"

Mack Wheeler's head whipped around. He scrutinized Harrigan's face and exclaimed, "Hey! You're that guy! I saw you in the Silver Palace last night, and I was wondering the same thing when I saw you handling those ruffians. Are you a professional fighter?"

Del shook his head. "No."

"Well, it was damn—oh, excuse me, ma'am—it was pretty obvious you've done some fighting somewhere. You made those Rebels look like lead-footed stumblebums."

"We also heard about the gunfight you had with them outside in the street, and how you protected the marshal from getting killed," put in Bittner. "You're certainly not dressed like a lawman, and I don't see a badge, but are you by chance a law officer of some kind?"

Harrigan smiled and shook his head again. "No. I learned to handle guns and to defend myself with my hands during the war. I was with a special unit of fighting men."

"Last night we heard you say that it was the Union side you fought on."

"Yes."

Linna Bittner cocked her head and assessed the tall man sitting opposite her. "Correct me if I am wrong, Mr. Harrigan, but it is my guess you were an officer."

Harrigan smiled pleasantly. "Why do you say that, ma'am?"

"You just have that air about you. Am I right?"

"Yes, ma'am. I was a captain. I served under Brigadier General Stephen A. Hurlbut in the Army of the Tennessee, which for a good part of the war was under the direct command of General Ulysses S. Grant."

Will Stubbs quickly straightened and his eyes widened. Swiveling around on the seat and thrusting his face toward Harrigan, he gasped, "You, sir, were in the Fourth Division under Hurlbut?"

"Yes, I was."

Shaking his head in astonishment, the silver-haired man declared, "Well, I'll be switched! That was the most famous division in the Civil War! The 'Fighting Fourth,' that's what they called you. You fellas went right into the teeth of artillery, gatlings, rifles, pistols, bayonets, and anything else the Confederates could throw at you—and still you spilled more southern blood than they'd ever admit. Why, you fellas made your mark everywhere you went to battle . . . Arkansas, Tennessee, Georgia, Virginia. Why, I—"

"You know an awful lot about us, Mr. Stubbs," cut in Harrigan. "Are you an historian of some kind?"

Stubbs grinned. "Nope, newspaper editor. I worked for the *Cincinnati Daily News* for thirty-one years. Just retired this past month, as a matter of fact. During the war I was editor of the war news department, so I edited a lot of stories written by our war correspondents on the grand and glorious exploits of the 'Fighting Fourth' Division."

The other passengers listened with great interest, astounded as the old gentleman reeled off battles, dates, weather conditions, casualty statistics, commanding officers of both sides, and other related facts of the Civil War. He proved to be a genuine fanatic on the subject of the Fourth Division of the Union Army of the Tennessee, and after recounting for several minutes the military successes of that division, Stubbs paused and then said, "But the most spectacular unit within the Fourth was the one comprised of those rough, tough leatherheads known as the Rangers. Yes, that's it! Hurlbut's Rangers!"

Harrigan folded his arms across his muscular chest and eased back in the seat. Stroking his mustache, he asked with a glimmer of amusement, "You know a lot about the Rangers, do you, Mr. Stubbs?"

"Oh, yes!" the old man replied excitedly. "Whooie! You talk about a fighting bunch! They'd sneak right into Confederate camps, quietly kill the sentries with their bare hands, and kidnap the commanding officers. They had the top brass in Richmond pulling their hair out!"

"You've sure got a good memory for details, Mr. Stubbs," Harrigan replied.

Nodding in agreement, Stubbs responded, "Yep, that's why I was such a good editor all those years. But my age has caught up with me, and sometimes things slip by me. Like right now."

"What do you mean?"

Putting his fingertips to his temples, Stubbs looked down at the coach floor and mumbled, "I'm trying to remember the name of the Rangers' leader. He was a captain. Let's see . . . uh . . . Captain . . . uh . . . Captain Harrison. Nope, that isn't it. Uh . . . Houligan. Nope, that's not right, either. Let's see . . . Captain . . ." His head snapped up and his eyes widened. "Captain Delbert Wade Harrigan!" he exclaimed, snapping his fingers. "You! I thought your name rang a bell after these young people mentioned your heroic deeds last night. You're the leader of Hurlbut's Rangers!"

Grinning proudly, Harrigan acknowledged, "That's me."

Stubbs grabbed Harrigan's right hand with both of his and shook it excitedly. "Am I ever honored to meet you, son!" Looking at the Bittners, he exclaimed, "No wonder he tore those oafs up last night! This fella is an absolute fighting machine!"

The old newspaperman continued to recount exploit after exploit of Hurlbut's Rangers, explaining excitedly that it was an elite fighting group of some twenty men whose primary function was to take Confederate camps by surprise. Stubbs elaborated further: Upon arriving at a camp, the Rangers would quietly eliminate each sentry by snapping his spinal cord while holding a hand over his mouth. Then, with machinelike precision, the unit would make their way to officers' tents, take the men captive, and bring them back to the Union camps as prisoners. When the rest of the soldiers found their sentries dead and their officers missing, they would become demoralized and disorganized.

Knowing it was the polite thing to do, Linna Bittner had tried to appear interested in hearing about the work of Hurlbut's Rangers. But she cringed when she listened to how men's necks had been snapped. And when Harrigan further explained how hands could be turned into lethal weapons, his graphic descriptions made Linna's skin crawl. She was thankful when the conversation finally trailed off, and she found herself staring curiously at Del Harrigan, wondering what he now did for a living. She and her husband had exchanged knowing looks when he first arrived at the stage depot, suspecting that the man was a gambler, and she was sure by the way the other two men looked at Harrigan that they, too, were wondering and guessing. However, nobody had the courage to ask directly.

Suddenly the coach started slowing down, and Linna peered out the window to see why. She was relieved to see that they had reached a swing station—the first since leaving Sioux City some three hours earlier—where the stationmaster would change horses and the passengers could get out and stretch their legs.

All too soon they were headed west across the Dakota plains once again. Linna Bittner settled back in her seat, and when the three men began pumping Harrigan for more stories about his war exploits, she grew weary of the subject and let her gaze drift over the broad expanse of hills and grass. She noticed that the grass was turning a pale, lifeless color and wondered vaguely if there had been any rain of late.

About an hour after they had started up again, Linna found herself growing drowsy from the rocking motion of the coach, and she soon drifted off to sleep. She awoke with a start when the stage rolled to a stop at the Butterfield depot in the center of a small town, where the passengers could have a meal in a restaurant.

Alighting from the stagecoach, the passengers walked in a group to a somewhat run-down café, where they sat together around a large table and ate. During the meal, Albert Bittner looked across the table and commented, "Mr. Harrigan, you've obviously seen some pretty bloody battles."

"You can say that again," Harrigan confirmed with a nod.

"What were some of the bloodiest?"

"Albert!" cut in Linna. "Maybe Mr. Harrigan is tired of talking about war and killing and all that."

Del Harrigan grinned. "I don't mind answering your

31

husband's questions, ma'am. War is something that men just naturally find fascinating."

Linna wanted to say that she minded hearing the answers, but she kept it to herself, and she tried to block out Harrigan's words when he answered, "One of the worst battles was when the Rangers fought along with the rest of the Army of the Tennessee when it besieged Nashville in early November of sixty-four. We had the city surrounded for over two weeks, but the rain came down so bad, we couldn't attack. Finally on the morning of the sixteenth we moved in. By midafternoon we had pushed the boys in gray into the Tennessee River, and it was like shooting ducks in a pond. The water was virtually red."

Linna screwed up her face and looked at the ceiling.

"Was Nashville the worst, Mr. Harrigan?" asked her husband.

"No. The worst was the battle of Shiloh in April of sixty-two."

"Wasn't that the battle where Confederate General A. S. Johnston was killed?" queried Will Stubbs, speaking with a mouthful of mashed potatoes.

Harrigan nodded, sipped coffee, and replied, "Yes. He got shot in the knee and bled to death."

Linna cringed.

Stubbs remarked, "I remember working on that story. It was said that the bodies of soldiers were so numerous on the battlefield when it was over that a man could walk across it and never set foot on the ground."

"That's exactly the way it was," responded Harrigan. "It looked like—"

"Mr. Harrigan, *please!*" interjected Linna. "I realize you enjoy discussing all this horror, but can we possibly talk about something else?"

"I'm sorry, ma'am," Harrigan apologized, his face coloring. "I was only trying to satisfy the curiosity of these men. But let me say that I do not enjoy killing and bloodshed, and except when someone asks me, I never talk about the war. I haven't been forced to kill anyone since then until last night—and believe me, I hope I'll never have it forced on me again." He smiled gently, adding, "I promise that from here on in, we men will talk about something else."

Linna sighed. "Thank you. I would very much appreciate it."

The conversation turned to how they all thought the rest of the journey would be, and soon they had finished their meal. Returning to the Butterfield station, Linna Bittner was delighted to find that a woman about the same age as she—early twenties—was joining the passengers. She was glad that she would have another woman to talk to and that she would no longer be the only female riding the coach, which had so far made her feel quite awkward. However, she did not care for the excessive way Helen Coffman was painted and dressed—nor for the way she acted toward the men when they were introduced. But her fears were soon dispelled when she realized that from the first moment that Helen had looked at Del Harrigan, she had eyes only for him and had no interest in Albert Bittner.

The sunlight danced on Helen's upswept copper-colored hair as she turned to the tall, handsome man after the introductions were made and told him with a bright smile, "You sure know how to dress, sugar. I bet I know what you do for a living."

Watching him carefully, Linna thought that Harrigan seemed uncomfortable under Helen's piercing gaze. He undoubtedly found her pretty, for no one could argue that fact, but he gave the impression that he did not care for her forwardness. Linna found herself wondering why the woman wore so much powder, rouge, and paint that she looked like a doll. And while Helen certainly had a wonderful hourglass figure, the tight-fitting, low-cut lavender dress she wore flaunted it to the point of bad taste.

Harrington did not acknowledge Helen's comment. Rather, he casually said to everyone, "We'd better get aboard, folks. I think our driver is eager to get rolling—as I'm sure we all are."

Albert boarded first and helped his wife in, and then

Helen stepped inside. "Why don't you sit next to me?" Linna suggested. "I've heard nothing but male voices since Sioux City."

Helen glanced sidelong at the Bittners and smiled. "Suits me just fine. Then I'll have a nice clear view of that good-looking fellow—from the tip of that gorgeous black hair to the bottom of those polished black boots."

Though appalled at Helen's boldness, Linna managed to hold her tongue.

Will Stubbs climbed on board, taking the far side of the opposite seat, and then Mack Wheeler settled in. This left Del Harrigan the seat next to the door, opposite the gregarious redhead, who smiled delightedly at her good fortune.

As the stage started up, Linna turned toward Helen Coffman and smiled. "Well, we'll be spending a lot of time together, so perhaps we might get acquainted. My husband and I are journeying home to Rapid City. We've been back east for a month, visiting with my parents, and I must say that while it was nice to see them again, it'll be good to get home. It's funny how after just a few years of marriage, home becomes the place where you share your life with your husband—not the place where you grew up. How about you, Miss Coffman—it is *Miss* Coffman, isn't it? I hope you don't think me rude or prying, but would you tell me a bit about yourself?"

Without taking her eyes off Harrigan, Helen replied tartly, "Yeah, it's 'miss,' all right, and there isn't much to tell." She leaned forward slightly on the seat, revealing even more of her well-endowed bosom, and huskily said to Harrigan, "I may seem a little brash, Del, but are *you* married?"

Obviously taken aback, and looking most uncomfortable under the intense scrutiny of Helen's green eyes, Harrigan shifted slightly in his seat and replied, "No, ma'am."

Helen sighed and sat back. "Good!" she declared, smiling. "I'll enjoy the ride even better now."

Nonplussed by the woman's brazenness—in particular at the rapidity with which she used Del Harrigan's given name—Linna gave her husband a quick look. Clearing her throat, she then made another attempt to get Helen into a womanly conversation, but Helen Coffman would have none of it. She had apparently made up her mind to focus all her attention on Del Harrigan and directed her conversation solely toward him.

Linna sat listening to the bold redhead, growing ever more impatient with her obliviousness to Harrigan's obvious discomfort. But Helen kept throwing herself at him. Finally Linna could take no more, and she interrupted her in the middle of a sentence and tried again to distract her. "How far are you going, Miss Coffman?"

Still staring hungrily at Harrigan—who, in turn, was staring pointedly out the window—the redhead batted her eyes and replied, "Well, I'm supposed to be starting a new job as a card dealer at the saloon up in Presho . . . but now I'm thinking of just staying on till Del gets off." She sighed and sat back in her seat. "I think I'd like to be wherever he is."

Chapter Four

It was nearing noon, and the town of Red Buffalo was baking under the blazing July sun. The slight breeze that sifted through town did little to ease the heat and brought only the smallest relief to its citizens.

Mabel Kipling, a dumpy woman of forty-seven, was hurrying along a street in the residential section as fast as her short legs would carry her. As much as she could, she kept to the shade provided by the oaks, elms, and cottonwoods that lined the street. Turning into the neat yard of a small white house, she walked up the short pathway and stepped onto the porch. She knocked on the door, and when there was no response, she knocked again. Finally she peered in through the parlor window but saw no one.

Shaking her head, Mabel sighed and stepped off the porch, walking around to the back of the house. But at the sight of the empty yard, she shrugged her shoulders, sighed again, and headed toward the street. She was about to start back to the center of town when a female voice called from a window of the house next door, "Mrs. Kipling! Oh, Mrs. Kipling!"

The portly woman halted and squinted at the face at the open window. "Oh, good afternoon, Mrs. Gladden."

"Good afternoon. Were you looking for Ginny Wheeler?"

"Yes. Do you know where I might find her?"

"She's at the schoolhouse. She left quite early this morning—I believe she said she had some painting to do."

Mabel thanked the neighbor for the information and,

36

sighing yet again at the additional exertion she would now have to endure, headed for the Red Buffalo schoolhouse at the south end of town.

It took Mabel Kipling some ten minutes to reach her destination, and when she finally puffed her way down the front walk of the schoolyard, she noticed that Ginny had all the windows and the front and side doors open; it was no doubt stifling inside. Mabel shook her head in astonishment. Even this heat did not stop the dedicated young woman from doing what she felt needed to be done.

Everyone in Red Buffalo loved beautiful Ginny Wheeler. She taught the children well and took her job seriously, which was appreciated by parents and children alike. Mabel knew that Ginny could have asked for help from the men in the community to paint the schoolhouse, but she had chosen to handle the job herself. Mabel figured the young teacher had done so because it was a way to keep her mind occupied—and Ginny Wheeler certainly needed that.

When Mabel entered the building and crossed the room, the wooden flooring creaked. Ginny was standing on a stepladder, painting the wall above the blackboard behind her desk, and at the sound of Mabel's footfalls, she looked around.

"Oh, hello, Mabel," she said, smiling and brushing back a loose curl of wavy brunette hair. "Is there something I can do for you?"

Mabel Kipling looked admiringly at the woman who was exactly twenty years younger—and probably a good fifty pounds lighter—than herself. Petite, with a figure that was the envy of most of the women in Red Buffalo, Ginny had a warm personality, a magnetic smile, and charm to spare. She also had a host of male admirers, and the most persistent of them was Frank Meeker, who was a year older than the captivating schoolteacher.

"I need to ask a favor of you, my dear," replied Mabel, still catching her breath.

Ginny stuck out her lower lip and blew at the stray lock of hair that insisted on dangling over her eyes. Running her forearm over her sweating brow, she responded, "Sure. What is it?"

"You are planning to go to the church picnic this evening, aren't you?"

"Reluctantly," replied Ginny, nodding. "Usually our picnics are happy occasions, but since this is also our farewell event for Reverend Burke, I'm not at all looking forward to it."

"I know what you mean, my dear. It's hard to let him and Mrs. Burke leave the congregation after all these years, but we do have to look at it from their point of view. They're getting along in years and they need a rest."

"I know," Ginny sighed, "but we've all grown to love them so much. And I for one will miss their advice terribly." Laying down the paintbrush and stepping down from the ladder, she wiped the sweat off again and sighed, "We'll never have another pastor nearly as good as Cletus Burke."

Moving closer, the stocky woman cautioned, "Now, you don't know that, Ginny. Maybe the new minister we're getting will surprise you. He certainly comes to us with a good recommendation from Reverend Burke and from the pastorate where he used to serve. I'm sure after some adjusting we will love him just as much."

"It's too bad he's a widower, though," Ginny mused. "It's hard to imagine a pastor without a wife at his side to help organize all the church social events."

"Well, who knows, maybe the good Lord will provide him with another wife."

Ginny sighed again. "Maybe—but I still wish Reverend Burke weren't leaving us." She shook her head. "At any rate, what was the favor you needed, Mabel?"

"Oh! I almost forgot. I was supposed to bake four pies for the picnic, and the door of my oven just fell off. One of the hinges is completely broken, and Harold won't be able to fix it in time for me to bake this afternoon. But I didn't realize you were doing this painting, so I'll see if I can get someone else to help out."

Blowing the stubborn wisp of hair away from her eyes

again, Ginny assured the portly woman, "That won't be necessary, Mabel. I can do it. I'll only be working another couple of hours here, and then I'll be able to bake the pies."

Mabel's brow furrowed. "You're sure that's not putting too much on you?"

"Not at all. I'll take care of it."

Mabel grinned. "Well, I won't argue with you. Thanks, Ginny." She started toward the door but then halted. Turning around, she asked softly, "I don't suppose you've heard anything from Mack?"

Ginny's delicate features hardened. "No."

Taking two steps back toward the schoolteacher, the portly woman said, "My dear, it simply isn't fair. You're young and very attractive—you should be enjoying life with some fine and good husband who loves you. Instead, here you are living alone, leading a dismal life."

A tentative smile touched Ginny's full lips. "I assure you my life isn't dismal, Mabel. I love teaching, and the children are my life now."

"But that's not enough, Ginny," countered Mabel. "A woman needs a husband, and—"

"I don't need a husband like Mack," cut in the brunette. "I wish I had never married him. I'll take my dismal life, as you put it, any day over what I had with him. I'm much better off with things as they are."

"But life goes by so quickly. You need to love and be loved while you're young. Certainly if your husband has deserted you, you ought to divorce him. There are plenty of fine young men around. Why, Frank Meeker—"

"Mabel, dear," sighed Ginny, "you worry too much about me. I'm doing fine."

"But you work so hard, honey. I mean, in addition to your teaching job, you're baking pies and taking in washing to earn extra money. And look at you. Here you are painting this place by yourself. You ought to let the men around here do it before you work yourself to death."

"I'm not baking and taking in washing anymore, Mabel," Ginny told her friend. "I got Mack's debt at the saloon paid off last month. I tell you I'm doing fine. Now, you go on home and let me get back to my job. I'll see you at the picnic."

"You're a dear," Mabel declared, giving Ginny a quick hug before heading for the door once again.

A tall, lanky young man was about to enter just as she reached the door, and he stood aside to let her through.

"Howdy, Mrs. Kipling," the man said.

"Hello, Frank," Mabel responded pleasantly. Starting down the steps, she asked him over her shoulder, "You're going to the picnic, aren't you?"

"Wouldn't miss it for the world," the sandy-haired young man called as he started across the room. "Especially if I can talk Ginny into going with me."

Ginny ignored the remark and climbed back up the ladder. She picked up the brush, dipped it in the paint can, and resumed her work—although she found it hard to concentrate with Frank Meeker staring up at her.

Frank, the Butterfield agent in Red Buffalo, was head over heels in love with Ginny Wheeler, and he often told her so. A bit of a country jake, he was good-looking in a boyish sort of way—although Ginny found his appearance about as bland as she found his personality. She glanced down at him and found him gazing lovingly up at her, and she quickly turned away.

"How about coming down so I can take you in my arms?" he asked hopefully.

Ginny kept painting, saying evenly, "Frank, it's so uncomfortably hot. The last thing in the world I need is to have your warm, sticky arms around me."

Pouting, he asked, "Ginny, when are you going to give in? I'm determined to win your love—you know that."

Sighing deeply, she replied caustically, "Indeed I do. All too well." Hearing the harshness in her own words, she added, more softly, "Frank, we've been over this a dozen times. I am not ready to fall in love again. I'm still hurting over my husband, and it's going to take time for me to get over it. A *lot* of time."

"You're not giving yourself a chance," he complained. "You should forget that . . . that no-good whelp, and put your life back together."

Dipping the brush again, Ginny blew the unruly wisp out of her eyes and countered, "I have forgotten Mack. As far as loving him, that died when he deserted me—but the wounds are still fresh, and they'll need time to heal. It may be years—or perhaps never—before I'm ready to trust a man enough to fall in love again."

Meeker was not easily discouraged. Smiling with assurance, he declared, "I'll make you forget those wounds, Ginny. I'll make you fall in love with me."

Ginny Wheeler's strokes became short and brisk as she concentrated intently on the painting, deliberately not responding to Frank's words.

He waited a moment and then asked, "Can I pick you up for the church picnic this evening?"

The beautiful brunette did not really want to go to the picnic with Meeker, but in order to get rid of him for the moment, she gave in. "All right, Frank. I'll be ready at six-thirty."

Grinning broadly, Meeker chirped, "Okay! See you then!" Almost skipping, he left the confines of the hot building.

After Meeker had gone, Ginny started painting the final wall. In her solitude, she relived her three-year marriage to Mack Wheeler—a marriage that had started with so much promise and ended with so much despair. She had gone to the altar with him feeling that she had found the man of her dreams, for he seemed so energetic, resourceful, and industrious. He had opened his own carpentry shop, and it appeared that it was going to do well. But the business and the marriage went sour almost from the beginning.

Mack was keeping busy with jobs, yet there seemed to be no money. They had been married only a month when Ginny learned what was happening to his earnings, discovering to her sorrow that Mack was an habitual gambler. After a heated battle over his gambling, Mack had shown remorse, begging for Ginny's forgiveness and promising to stay away from the gambling haunts. The vow lasted exactly four days. Again he seemed repentant, promising to overcome his weakness. He knew he was wrong, but he could stick to his pledge if only Ginny would stay with him.

Ginny Wheeler loved her husband and wanted to make their marriage work, but she saw it was going to take time for Mack to conquer the vice that, she learned, had begun when he was only fourteen years old. She would have to work to make ends meet. Educated as a teacher, Ginny took the job of schoolmistress in Red Buffalo.

Things went from bad to worse. Soon Mack did not bother working at all but instead spent all his time in the saloons at the gaming tables—where he was always going to "strike it rich." Ginny's small salary was all they had, and he was stealing even that and gambling it away.

One night he did not come home. He made a lame excuse when he came in at dawn, but Ginny knew he had been with another woman. She confronted him, and he admitted his indiscretion, again begging her forgiveness. She forgave him. The same thing happened again—and she forgave him again. It happened so often that she lost count of the number of times he had promised to reform. For three years Mack kept them poor with his gambling losses. For three years, trying to keep house and home together, Ginny took in washing in addition to her teaching job. And for three years, Mack kept promising to quit gambling and carrying on with other women. It never happened.

The marriage grew steadily worse until finally, some six months before, Mack ran off with a saloon girl, leaving a note saying he would send Ginny her divorce papers. They never arrived. He also left behind a substantial gambling debt at the Black Diamond Saloon, and although it was not her responsibility, Ginny repaid the entire amount over a period of five months. She earned additional wages by baking pies for the Great Plains Café in town.

Ginny Wheeler was having a hard time trying to control the hatred that had built up inside her toward the man who had treated her so badly. Knowing that hatred would eat at her soul like a cancer, she had talked with Reverend Burke about it and had prayed that God would help her to be rid of it. But whenever Mack came to her mind, the battle raged anew within her.

Ginny finished the final wall and closed the lid on the paint can. Checking the clock on the back wall, she decided she still had enough time to paint the big potbellied stove that sat in the middle of the room before heading for home. Placing the paintbrush she had been using into a container of kerosene, she then opened a can of stove black and, using a smaller brush, recoated the stove that was the source of heat for the schoolhouse.

Finally she finished the job and closed up the schoolhouse, heading for home. As she walked she told herself that what she had told Mabel Kipling was the truth: She loved her job and she adored the children, who seemed to adore her in turn. Teaching them gave her life real purpose, and she found a balm for her injured heart in their love. Although she would not call herself happy, she at least felt content . . . and that was quite a bit more than she had felt all during her three-year marriage to Mack Wheeler.

At six o'clock, Frank Meeker closed up the Butterfield office and drove to Ginny Wheeler's house with a broad smile on his face all the way. Leaping down from his buggy, he bounded up the pathway and onto the porch and knocked impatiently on the door, calling, "Ginny? Anybody home?"

Ginny's soft voice called from the kitchen, "Come on in, Frank."

Meeker followed his nose. The smell of freshly baked pies permeated the house. Sniffing loudly as he entered the kitchen, he looked at the pies and exclaimed, "Ahh! Boy, would I like to come home to this kind of cooking every night. Especially if you were the one doing the cooking for me."

Ignoring his comment, Ginny closed a cupboard door and said, "The picnic basket is right there beside the table. If you'll carry it and the pie basket out to the buggy for me, I'll finish getting ready. I won't be but a minute."

As she spoke, the young brunette disappeared into her bedroom. Meeker shrugged his shoulders, picked up the two baskets, and headed out the door. Ginny had not yet come out by the time he laid them carefully in the buggy, so he went back inside the house to wait.

Ginny came out of her bedroom and stepped into the parlor, smoothing her ankle-length blue gingham dress. Pausing, she looked at Frank and then glanced toward the kitchen. "Did you get the baskets?"

"They're in the buggy," he replied, moving toward her. Suddenly he swept her into his arms in one smooth movement and, holding her close, breathed, "I'm crazy about you, Ginny. Please say you feel something for me."

Ginny quickly turned her head away from Meeker's probing mouth. Pushing herself free of his grasp, she said, "Frank, don't! Please remember I'm still a married woman. Can't we just be friends? I like you, and I think you're a fine man—but I am not in love with you. Please don't smother me!"

Looking sulky, Meeker argued, "The only thing that makes you a married woman is that you never received divorce papers from Mack. For all *practical* purposes, the marriage is over."

"Well, that may be," parried Ginny, moving to the door, "but until there is a legal divorce, I still consider myself to be Mack's wife." Halting at the door, she added, "Frank, we can either go on as friends, or we can end our relationship right now."

Meeker answered quickly, "All right, I'll try not to crowd you, Ginny." Sighing loudly to let her know that he was not thrilled at the prospect of being merely her friend, he escorted her down the pathway. "Come on. We'll be late for the picnic."

*   *   *

The setting sun had turned the surface of the White River to liquid gold as the picnic got under way on the riverbank a quarter mile from town. The one hundred and fifty men, women, and children comprising the membership of the Red Buffalo Community Church were gathered together. Before they began their meal, the children played games and the adults square danced for an hour to music provided by three men playing guitar, fiddle, and banjo. Despite the festivities, there was a touch of sadness to the occasion; this would be the last time the congregation would meet as a whole with its aging pastor, who would be leaving Red Buffalo almost immediately after his retirement.

The picnic broke up at nine-thirty, and at a quarter to ten, Frank Meeker pulled his buggy to a halt in front of Ginny Wheeler's house. Hopping out quickly, he ran around the vehicle and gave her his hand. When she stepped from the buggy, he folded her into his arms and tried to kiss her lips, but once more Ginny turned her face away and eluded him. Twisting from his grasp, she hurried to the house.

Meeker caught up with her and grasped her by the arm, pulling her to a stop. Jerking loose, Ginny looked at him in the dim light from the quarter moon and told him angrily, "Apparently we can't just be friends, Frank, so we might as well not see each other anymore."

"But Ginny, I—"

"I told you I'm not ready for romance. If you can't understand that, we have nothing more to say." She turned and walked away.

"Okay, okay," he gasped.

Trying not to be unkind, she stopped and sighed, "Good night, Frank. I appreciate your taking me to the picnic." Then she quickly stepped onto the porch and opened the door.

"Ginny!" called Meeker.

When she turned around and looked at him, he asked,

"If I swear to you that I won't try to kiss you until you say it's okay, can I see you again?"

"Let's talk about it later, Frank," she said wearily. "Right now I just want to get some rest. It's been a long day."

Backing toward his buggy, Meeker assured her, "I'll give you time, Ginny. I promise. I'll give you time."

The exhausted young woman stepped into her house and closed the door. Leaning back against it, she half whispered, "No matter how much time goes by, Frank, I could never fall in love with you. You're a nice fellow, but you just don't move me. For that matter, maybe no one ever will." She sighed deeply. "But right now, I'm too tired to care."

Chapter Five

The unrelenting sun beat down upon the westbound stagecoach, turning it into a veritable oven and punishing the passengers inside. Although the prairie wind was picking up, the blasts of air did little more than throw dust through the open windows of the stifling coach.

Trying to exert themselves as little as possible, the passengers kept their conversation to a minimum and tried to ignore the heat and dust—except Helen Coffman. With a great deal of fuss, she took a fan from her purse and snapped it open, dramatically fanning her face, and then swearing under her breath when it did nothing to alleviate her discomfort. She ignored Linna Bittner, who was watching her with amusement from the corner of her eye, and merely stuffed the fan back in her purse and pulled out a large compact. Using a powder puff, she dabbed away sweat beads and labored at keeping her makeup just right. Blowing dust from the mirror in the compact—which she was satisfied to note floated onto Linna's lap—the redhead applied a fresh coat of lip rouge.

Carefully observing her mouth in the mirror, Helen worked her lips to spread the color evenly. When she was satisfied with the results, she closed the compact and—to her delight—found the handsome Del Harrigan watching her. Refusing to consider that it might be nothing more than idle curiosity, Helen decided his attention was ample proof of his interest in her. She batted her eyes and gave him a provocative smile, but to her chagrin, he quickly looked away.

Perturbed that he did not flirt back and that she had not immediately won him over, she covered her disappointment by snapping open the compact again and repowdering her face. Looking over at Harrigan, she asked seductively, "Do I look all right, sugar?"

Harrigan stared at her for a moment. "You look fine, ma'am," he told her tightly.

Oblivious to the fact that she had backed him into a corner and that to have ignored her would have been rude, she was thrilled at his response. She smiled coyly at him and insisted, "You don't have to call me *ma'am*, honey. Just call me Helen."

"Yes, ma'am," he replied offhandedly, and then immediately turned to the old man to his left to engage him in conversation.

Not being the least bit interested in what Will Stubbs had to say, but wanting to impress Harrigan, Helen listened to their discussion for a few moments. The old man was saying how excited he was to be moving in with his daughter and son-in-law, and how much he looked forward to being able to watch his three grandchildren grow. Becoming bored, she finally dropped the pretense and sat back in her seat, gazing out the window at the flat Dakota landscape until she nodded off.

The wind was still whipping across the plains as the stagecoach pulled into the small town of Kimball in midafternoon. The coach rolled to a stop at the Butterfield home station, which was located near the end of the block adjacent to a trading post that also housed a saloon. Dust devils whirled every which way, throwing dirt into the faces of man and beast.

Del Harrigan was the first to alight from the coach and Helen Coffman was next, giving her hand to the tall, handsome man as she leaned into the doorway and stepped out. When her feet touched the ground, she did not let go of Harrigan's hand. Instead, drawing close to him, she

48

looked up and smiled. "You really are an incredibly attractive man, Del, and you absolutely set my heart to beating."

Harrigan's face reddened. Awkwardly pulling his hand free, he hurriedly removed his hat and shook the dust from it.

When Linna Bittner hopped down, she looked from Helen's face to Harrigan's and back again and quickly assessed the situation. She took the redhead by the arm, firmly guiding her toward the back of the station in the direction of the privies. "Come, Helen, we don't have much time. The stage will be pulling out before we know it."

While the other passengers headed in the same direction, Del Harrigan stood and watched as the driver, shotgunner, and station agent began unhitching the tired horses. When they had nearly finished, he engaged them in conversation.

"I believe we're getting into Sioux country now, aren't we?"

Chuckling, the agent replied, "You've been in Sioux country ever since you pulled out of Sioux City, mister. Of course, they're ordinarily a little thicker from here west."

"Been any trouble from them lately?"

"No, sir. Things have been pretty quiet in all of Dakota Territory since the massacre at the Little Big Horn late last month. Actually, Crazy Horse and Sitting Bull have concentrated most of their fighting forces in Wyoming and Montana since the beginning of June, so to my knowledge, white folks haven't really been bothered in Dakota Territory since then."

Nodding, Harrigan commented, "I'm relieved to hear that." He paused and looked around, observing, "By the way, it seems to me that the farther west we go, the drier it gets. Though the grass is at least a foot high, it's completely parched. Is this normal?"

Shaking his head, the agent replied, "The grass is as high as it is because we had some good spring rains, but it hasn't rained in weeks."

Harrigan pivoted as a dust devil whirled into him,

49

and then he mused, "With it this dry, the danger of prairie fire must be running high."

"That it is, Mr. Harrigan," the driver agreed. "I can guarantee you that everybody in these parts is keepin' his eyes peeled."

"We've already had some small fires in the area," added the agent. "They're usually started by heat lightning. But ordinarily we can get them under control pretty quick—that is, unless the wind is blowing hard."

"You mean like it is right now?"

The agent looked up at the tall man and grinned. Shaking his head with amusement, he declared, "You must be from back east."

"Pennsylvania," confirmed Harrigan. "Why?"

"If you were from around here, you wouldn't call this little breeze a wind. If you stick around a day or two, you'll find out what real wind is."

"Then I guess I'll be getting educated," said Harrigan. "I'm on my way to take up residence in Red Buffalo."

"Red Buffalo?" echoed the agent. "Well, you'll find out, all right."

The driver and shotgunner eyed each other, grinning, but made no comment. Wondering just what he had in store, Del Harrigan took his leave of the three men to take his turn at the privy.

As the passengers returned from the privies and waited while fresh horses were harnessed to the stagecoach, they lolled in the shade of the porch overhang, sitting on wooden benches. A number of local people were stopping in at the saloon, made particularly thirsty by the intense heat.

Enjoying the relative cool under the canopy, Helen Coffman fanned herself while keeping a close eye on Del Harrigan. She admired the way he stood so tall and straight and wondered how much muscle was hidden under his coat. From the way the garment fit his wide shoulders and his upper arms, she guessed he was solidly built. The man was utterly fascinating.

Helen was trying to think of a way to get his attention

when three scruffy men emerged from the saloon and looked around. The redhead eyed them sharply. One of them was an ugly bear of a man who, judging from his clothing, appeared to be a trapper. He was dressed in dirty buckskins and wore a broad-brimmed hat that was so dirty and sweat-stained, one could not detect its original color. Helen was sure he stank to high heaven. There was a long-barreled revolver holstered on his waist, and a knife was sheathed on his belt. A flicker of a smile graced Helen's lips as she decided that this repulsive man might be just the means of getting the handsome Mr. Harrigan to concentrate on her.

Looking furtively around to make sure Harrigan did not see what she was doing, she waited until the huge trapper spied her, and then she gave him a flirtatious smile, licking her lips and lowering her eyes provocatively. The ruse worked, for the man said something to his two companions and then walked slowly toward her, eyeing her boldly.

Pressing his unwashed body close to hers, he told her suggestively, "I'll bet you came in on that stage—which means you've probably had a long, lonesome journey. If you're lookin' to have a good time, pretty lady, ol' Gus can sure as hell give it to you." He leaned down, his foul breath assaulting Helen's nostrils, and added hoarsely, "Tell you what, honey, why don't you just leave the stage and come ride with me?"

Looking up at him scornfully, Helen squealed, "Leave me alone!"

The man was playing right into Helen's hands. Pressing closer, he grasped the redhead's shoulders and growled, "I said let's me and you go ridin', honey."

Helen twisted in his grasp and screamed loudly, "Get your filthy hands off me, you big ape! You're hurting me!"

Everyone turned and looked Helen's way, including Del Harrigan. While the trapper got angrier and angrier, Helen struggled to free herself and shouted for help.

True to his nature, Harrigan barked at the man, "Hey! Let go of the lady, mister!"

Ignoring the intrusion, the trapper made another lewd comment to Helen.

Harrigan rushed to Helen's defense, curtly declaring, "The lady obviously doesn't want your company. Now leave her alone."

The trapper's ponderous head snapped around, and he regarded Harrigan with a sneer. "You gonna make me?"

"Yeah," rasped Harrigan, stubbornly jutting his jaw.

Helen was thrilled. His response proved that the handsome devil really did care about her.

Seizing Helen's left wrist, Gus looked at her hand. Then he glared at Harrigan and announced, "There ain't no weddin' ring on her finger, so I'm supposin' you ain't her husband." Defiantly, the trapper folded her in his powerful arms and hugged her to his smelly body. Ignoring Helen's shrieks, the man challenged Harrigan, "I ain't gonna let go of her till I'm good and ready."

Helen Coffman expected Del Harrigan to do something—but instead he stood scrutinizing the huge man. She worried that perhaps he realized that she had deliberately gotten herself into this situation, and that he was prepared to let her stew in her own juice and learn a lesson. But she quickly decided that he would not do that. Harrigan was a gentleman; he would not leave a lady to the mercy of this giant of a man. He would find it impossible to just turn and walk away.

Growing impatient, Helen shrieked, "Del, please help me! He's hurting me!"

Anger flared in Harrigan's eyes. Pointing stiffly at the trapper, he hissed, "Let go of her, mister, or you'll be sorry!" However, the look on his face said that he knew the warning would go unheeded. Making a move, he abruptly stepped around the pair, doubled up his fist, and drove a violent blow to Gus's left kidney. The giant howled, momentarily lifting Helen off the ground and whirling to meet his foe. But Harrigan had slipped behind him again and sent another blow to the man's other kidney. The pain was apparently too great, and Gus released Helen, rubbing at his back. Then, his face purple with fury, he roared like an angry grizzly bear and went after his challenger.

Helen quickly got out of the way, running to the safety of the other passengers, and eagerly watched the battle. Although Harrigan was very tall and muscular, compared to Gus he seemed almost puny.

Using his head like a battering ram, Harrigan bent over and thundered toward the enormous man converging on him, slipping through Gus's balled fists and slamming him hard in the middle of his massive chest. It was apparent that the impact was painful to Harrigan, but it also knocked the wind out of Gus. The trapper took a step back and gasped for breath, shaking his huge head.

Making the most of his advantage, Harrigan followed through with a mighty punch to Gus's nose, and the man's eyes watered instantly. Harrigan began retreating, but he did not move quite fast enough, and the trapper caught him on the side of the head with one of his hamlike fists, lifting him off the ground. As Harrigan landed in the dust, the trapper drew back his right foot and kicked. But the agile Harrigan dodged and, timing his move, reached out and seized the foot, giving it a savage twist. The trapper lost his footing and slammed hard against the ground, howling. Both men rose to their knees at the same time, each making a fist, but Harrigan beat Gus to the punch and belted him once again on the nose. The huge man fell backward and Harrigan stood up, gasping for air.

Fury mottled the trapper's filthy face, and he came again at Harrigan, fists balled. Harrigan ducked, then drove two violent punches to the huge man's stomach, doubling him over.

Helen Coffman felt Linna Bittner's eyes boring into her, and the redhead reluctantly turned away from the fight. From the side of her mouth, Linna asked, "Are you satisfied now, Helen?"

Looking at the young matron with feigned innocence, she replied, "Whatever are you talking about?"

"I watched you set this up—but I assure you, when it's over, you won't be any better off."

Helen raised her chin. "We'll see about that," she retorted tartly, and then once again excitedly watched the combatants.

There was a glazed look in the trapper's eyes as he stood up once again. Breathing hard, he shook his big head, as if trying to get rid of the pain.

Harrigan barreled in and gave Gus two more strong punches, one on his bleeding nose and another to his stomach. The trapper responded by wrapping his arms around the smaller man and wrestling him to the ground.

As they watched the two men roll over and over, everyone seemed to know that Harrigan would have to end the fight soon, for while he had the advantage in agility and speed, the trapper obviously had it all over him in strength.

Suddenly Harrigan locked his hands around his opponent's big right arm, bending it up behind his back and jerking it hard. The smaller man puffed, "You can let this come to an end without getting hurt, mister. Just say you're through, and I'll let go."

Unwilling to give in, Gus gnashed his teeth and bawled, "I'm gonna kill you!"

The other passengers knew that Del Harrigan had no choice when he wrenched the man's arm savagely, dislocating the shoulder. The trapper screamed in agony and fell down as Harrigan released him. Forcing himself to his feet, swearing vehemently, Gus reached for the revolver in his holster.

Harrigan rushed in and slammed the man's jaw so hard that it lifted him off the ground, and he landed with a heavy thud and lay motionless. His two friends darted to him, kneeling down and trying to revive him.

Gasping for breath, Del Harrigan pivoted around slowly and looked toward his friends. Helen rushed to him, snatching up his fallen hat, and exclaimed, "Oh, darling! You did it all for me! My hero!"

Before Harrigan could protest, Helen wrapped her

arms around him and kissed him soundly on the lips. When she let go of him, he was clearly embarrassed, although the redhead chose to believe he was merely being shy in front of the others.

Suddenly Will Stubbs tapped Helen's shoulder and told her, "Excuse me, ma'am. We need to help Mr. Harrigan over to the water trough and get him cleaned up."

"Oh, of course! How thoughtful of you. I'll help."

As they started toward the trough, the trapper's two cohorts looked angrily at Harrigan but said nothing. They undoubtedly felt it was Gus's fight, not theirs, and wisely decided to stay out of it.

When the passengers reboarded the stage a few minutes later, Helen proudly sat next to Harrigan and slipped her arm inside his. She poured out her gratitude for his having come to her rescue, but Harrigan merely looked uncomfortable. To Helen's obvious dismay, he said not a word to her during the entire ride to Chamberlain, where passengers and crew would spend the night.

Darkness was already blanketing the prairie when the stagecoach drove into Chamberlain. Met by his family, Will Stubbs bade the other passengers good-bye and then rode away smiling happily with one grandchild on each side of him and one in his lap.

The remaining passengers ate together in the dining room of the hotel where they were staying. During the meal, Helen Coffman did her best to charm the handsome man she was so smitten with, but while Harrigan was polite to her, he remained aloof.

After dining, the passengers bade each other good night and went to their rooms, all of which were on the second floor. Helen Coffman's room was next door to that of the Bittners, and while Albert was readying himself for bed, Linna slipped into the hallway and went to speak with her.

Linna's knock was answered quickly, and from the

crestfallen look on Helen's face, it was clear that she had expected it to be Del Harrigan at her door.

"May I speak with you a moment?" asked Linna.

Sighing, Helen shrugged. "Sure," she said tonelessly, folding her arms across her chest.

Linna got right to the point. Looking the woman straight in the eye, she declared, "You ought to leave Mr. Harrigan alone. It's as plain as day that he's not attracted to you, and furthermore, you only make him extremely uncomfortable when you push yourself on him. Besides, unless you're blind, you can see that your little escapade this afternoon was useless."

Helen's painted face settled into a hard, indignant mask. "I don't see that it's any of your business, Mrs. Bittner!" she snapped. "But since you've stuck your little upturned nose into it, I'll tell you this: I fell in love with Del the first minute I laid eyes on him, and one way or another, I'll win him over."

"No, you won't," countered Linna. "You're not his type."

"Not his type?" Helen shot back. "Look, dearie, the man's obviously a gambler, and I've been around gamblers nearly all my life. I know how they think. Del and I will make a perfect couple."

"I've no doubt you know your way around gamblers— and the saloons they hang out in."

Helen's eyes flashed. Her hands went to her hips, where her fingers drummed an angry tattoo. "Well, let me tell you something, honey. I'm not one of those cheap women who drapes herself over every goggle-eyed man in the place! I am a respectable card dealer! For the past two years I've worked in a high-class casino, and I've been offered a job doing the same thing at a new casino that's just opened." Looking the Bittner woman up and down, she added, "You think you're better than me, is that it?"

"That's not it at all," replied Linna. "I wouldn't be standing here having this discussion with you except that Mr. Harrigan is such a nice man, and I don't like to see you driving him into a corner."

"He's a big boy," Helen rejoined sharply. "He can take care of himself. We all saw that back at Kimball, didn't we?"

"Against a *man*, yes. But he's too much of a gentleman to tell a woman to leave him alone, and you're taking advantage of that."

Helen waggled her head and said caustically, "Well, little miss guardian angel, you've failed to convince me. I am not going to leave him alone. I'm in love with the man, and I'm going to have him." She smiled smugly. "As I said, we'll make the perfect couple. The man is a professional gambler—anyone with a little worldly experience can see that—and I'm sure he's got money. He's either going to open up a new gambling place or take over an existing one, but I know a successful gambler when I see one." Her face grew cold, and she muttered, "Now, if you don't mind, I'd like to get my beauty sleep."

Linna turned on her heel and walked back to her room, and Helen closed the door. Leaning against it, she said half aloud, "As much as I hate to admit it, that meddlesome busybody may be right about one thing. Maybe I am pushing myself a bit too fast on Del. I'll just bide my time for a while. Then, after he's settled into town, one day I'll show up in Red Buffalo at his casino, and he and I will make beautiful music together."

Chapter Six

Helen Coffman came out of her room the next morning at the same time Del Harrigan emerged from his, holding his black leather valise. The flirtatious smile on her face was quickly replaced with an angry frown when Linna Bittner stepped into the hallway and brushed wordlessly by the redhead, her husband Albert in tow. Helen attempted to erase the expression on her face, but Harrigan had already seen the displeasure written there, and he wondered what had occurred between the two women. Deciding he really did not care what went on in this impudent woman's mind, he merely nodded to her and headed for the staircase.

"Del! Del, wait for me!" she called, taking quick, mincing little steps after him. "I thought we could breakfast together."

He quickly told himself it would be too rude to tell her that he had suddenly lost his appetite, and instead replied testily, "Suit yourself."

When they reached the bottom of the stairs, Helen boldly linked her arm in his, and together they entered the hotel restaurant. She deliberately paused in the entryway, making sure that the Bittners and Mack Wheeler saw them. Then she guided Harrigan over to the table where the three passengers were already seated. As all the other chairs were taken, Harrigan had no choice but to sit beside her, but he immediately struck up an animated conversation with the Bittners.

It was almost seven o'clock when the passengers walked over to the Butterfield office. Helen Coffman kept as close to Harrigan as she could, and he thought to himself that the stage could not get to her destination soon enough to suit him.

Just past noon Harrigan got his wish and the stage rolled into Presho, coming to a halt in front of the Butterfield office in the center of town. Pointing out the window to the Golden Slipper Saloon and Casino directly across the street, Helen Coffman announced to Harrigan, "That's where I'll be working if you want to come find me, Del."

Harrigan managed a noncommittal "Mm-hmm."

The Butterfield agent emerged from the office and opened the coach door, welcoming the passengers to Presho. Harrigan stepped out and, gentleman that he was, offered Helen his hand. She accepted it with a smile and alighted. She turned to give Linna Bittner a frosty glare as the couple stepped past her. Then she planted a smile back on her lips when she looked up at Harrigan. Still clinging to his hand, she told him, "Sugar, I want to thank you again for rescuing me from that horrid animal. Who knows what would have happened to little old Helen if you hadn't been there."

"I just did what had to be done, ma'am."

The redhead was about to speak again when a well dressed, middle-aged man approached and declared expansively, "Ah, Miss Coffman! I've been so looking forward to your arrival."

Helen turned and looked questioningly at the man; then recognition flooded her face. "Why, good afternoon, Mr. Kelly. Forgive me for not recognizing you right away. It's been such a trying journey, and this heat is quite fierce. . . ."

"I understand. Well, I'll bet you're anxious to get started."

She smiled fetchingly. "I am indeed. I'm also looking forward to earning some real money."

Laughing, Kelly answered her, "I'm sure with your

beauty, you'll draw men to the gambling tables like flies to honey."

"Why, Mr. Kelly," giggled the redhead, "you say the nicest things!" She suddenly put her hand to her mouth and then glanced up at the tall man whose arm she still held. "Oh, my, where are my manners! Lucas Kelly, I'd like you to meet Del Harrigan."

"It's a pleasure, Mr. Harrigan. Will you be staying here in Presho?"

Shaking his head forcefully, Harrigan extricated his arm from Helen's and told the saloon owner his destination.

The driver handed Helen's trunk down to the agent, and Lucas Kelly told him to send it over to the hotel, where she would be staying until other arrangements could be made. Then, offering Helen his arm, he told her, "Come on, I want to show you the place."

"Just one moment, Mr. Kelly," she replied, and then stepped close to Del Harrigan. Looking up into his eyes, she pouted slightly and told him, "I've dreaded this moment, darling. Let me be sure I understand, now. You *are* planning to live in Red Buffalo permanently, aren't you?"

A bit puzzled by her question, Harrigan answered lightly, "I am."

"Good," Helen commented with a wide smile. Taking him by surprise, the doll-faced woman planted a hasty kiss on his lips and then declared, "I'll see you again, sugar."

Thinking Helen was only being cordial, Harrigan replied politely, "Sure thing."

With a flourish, Helen Coffman took Lucas Kelly's arm and sashayed away, and when Harrigan turned and headed toward the Butterfield office, he shook his head and breathed a sigh of relief. Perhaps now he could relax for the rest of his journey.

While a fresh team was being hitched to the stage-coach, the Butterfield agent escorted two men from his office and introduced them to the other passengers. The newcomers—two businessmen in their fifties, Neal Jones and Wesley Sartin—were welcomed by their fellow travelers, and moments later the passengers climbed aboard the coach to continue the journey.

As the stage moved on, the discussion turned to the massacre of the Seventh Cavalry at the Little Big Horn River. Wesley Sartin commented, "I read just yesterday that President Grant has ordered the army at Fort Abraham Lincoln to put on an all-out effort to capture both Sitting Bull and Crazy Horse. The article said Grant and all the brass in Washington are really outraged over the massacre."

Nodding in agreement, Neal Jones put in, "The whole nation feels that way—at least every sensible person does. The loss of such a great leader as General Custer will leave its mark on our army, that's for sure."

Del Harrigan was aware that the Bittners were watching him carefully, waiting for him to comment, but although the temptation was strong to give his view of Custer's inexcusable flamboyance, he held his peace. It would serve no useful purpose.

Looking somewhat surprised at Harrigan's silence, Albert Bittner—who admired him greatly—proudly told the two newcomers about Harrigan's military background. When Jones and Sartin showed great interest, Linna sighed audibly.

"Oh, oh," she declared, half amused. "I have a feeling I know exactly the direction this conversation is going to take."

"My apologies, Mrs. Bittner," Harrigan told her. "We can speak of other matters, if you prefer."

She shook her head. "No, that's all right. You men enjoy yourselves; I'll just watch the scenery."

Thanking her, Jones and Sartin excitedly asked Harrigan all about his Union Army career.

They had traveled a few miles beyond Presho and were slowing down to make a sharp bend in the road, when suddenly gunshots were heard. Linna Bittner screamed, and the stagecoach jerked to a halt, almost throwing the passengers from their seats.

"Throw down your weapons!" a harsh voice demanded

of the driver and shotgunner. When Del Harrigan stuck his head out the window to see what was going on, a man on horseback snarled, "Back inside, mister! If I see your face come out that window again, I'll shoot it off!"

"Don't try anything, folks!" warned the driver, calling down. "Three armed men have got the drop on us!"

Harrigan pulled his head back inside and looked at the others. "They've got us cold," he told them glumly, noticing that Mack Wheeler's face had turned an ashen gray.

"You men are wasting your time," the driver nervously told the gunmen. "We're not carrying any money, just passengers."

"Money ain't what we're after," one of the gunmen growled. He walked over to the coach and pointed his cocked revolver inside the window. "All right!" he bawled. "Everybody out!"

Del Harrigan climbed down first, and then one by one the other passengers filed out behind him. Mack Wheeler, looking as though he were about to faint, held back, obviously wanting to be last to leave the coach.

Linna Bittner trembled uncontrollably, cowering beside her husband. Looking at the young matron, the gunman told her, "Don't worry, lady. We ain't gonna hurt you . . . unless somebody tries somethin' stupid."

As the passengers stood together, the gunman looked them over. Then he stepped beside the stagecoach and yanked the door wide open, aiming his pistol at the man cowering inside. "Come on out of there, Wheeler!" he growled. "Right now!"

Wheeler's body was shaking as he slid slowly across the seat toward the door. As he stepped from the coach, he accidentally bumped Del Harrigan's black valise, which slid off the seat and teetered unnoticed at the edge of the door.

Looking coldly at Wheeler, the leader of the trio announced, "You're the man we want."

Wheeler swallowed hard and licked his lips. "Wh-what do you want *me* for?"

The gunman snorted in derision. "Don't play dumb, Wheeler. You know damn well why we've come for you. And don't worry. We've even brought along an extra horse, so your ride back to Sioux City will be comfortable— and fast."

Wheeler licked his lips again, his eyes darting first to the faces of the gunmen and then to the bewildered faces of his fellow passengers. He looked at them pleadingly and then told them, "Honest, I don't know who these men are! You've got to help me!"

The leader stepped up to Wheeler, standing uncomfortably close. "I guess every time you gambled at the Silver Palace, you were too busy losin' money to notice us. Well, we work for Perry Prince—you remember him, don't you, Wheeler? The owner of the casino? Seems like you got real forgetful after you lost all that money, and you skipped town still owin' him five thousand dollars." He grabbed Wheeler's shirt, pulling the trembling man to within inches of his face. "Does that ring a bell, Wheeler?"

Mack Wheeler's face turned a pasty white. "P-please," he begged, "give me a chance to come up with the money. I'll pay it back, I promise I will. You've got to believe me! I always meant to pay Mr. Prince—heck, that's why I left Sioux City. I needed to get back home so I could get the money together." Fearfully, he added in a rush, "You've got to give me a chance! I own a house and some land in Red Buffalo, and I-I'll sell it and give all the money to Mr. Prince. Honest! And if that doesn't cover my debt, why I'll pack up my wife and we'll move to Sioux City. She's a schoolteacher, see, so we can both work and pay off the balance. Her income isn't large, but it's steady. Please, just give me a chance, okay?"

The gunman merely spat into the dirt. "Nope," he said flatly. "I'm to bring you back with me or kill you, one or the other . . . that is, unless you can come up with the five thousand plus the interest Mr. Prince has added on for your havin' skipped out on him. Your debt's up to six thousand, now. And the longer you go without payin', the higher the interest."

The expression on Del Harrigan's face showed little sympathy for a man who had gotten himself into a fix like this by gambling. But, clearly, he equally disliked the casino owner's tactics. He took a step toward the gunman, saying, "Look, mister, why don't you be reasonable? True, Mr. Wheeler was wrong to leave Sioux City when he owed your boss a great deal of money, but he's offered to make the debt right. You've got to at least give him a chance to do it."

Waving his revolver threateningly at Harrigan, the gunman walked toward him and muttered, "I don't have to do anything of the kind! And I'd advise you to stay out of this, if you know what's good for you!" He stared for a moment at the tall man and then angrily backhanded him across the face with his free hand.

Harrigan, touching his fingers to his stinging cheek, neither said nor did anything in response. Although he was obviously finding it hard not to knock the man flat, he also knew he would get a bullet for his trouble. However, the loud slap momentarily spooked the horses, which whinnied and jerked the stagecoach slightly. The sudden movement dislodged Harrigan's valise from the doorway and it tumbled to the ground.

It caught the leader's eye, and he turned and stared at Wheeler. "Now what do we have here? Is this full of cash, maybe?" Getting no reply, he walked over and picked up the fallen valise.

Harrigan suddenly snapped, "Keep your hands off that!"

Ignoring him, the gunman flipped the latches and yanked the case open. He rifled through the contents, finding little more than a few notes and papers plus a large black Bible. Lifting up the Bible for his cronies to see, he laughed and said, "Well, whaddya know? We've got us a holy man in this group!" Eyeing the initials on the outside of the valise, he walked over to Del Harrigan and sneered, "Since you're the one who hollered for me to keep my hands off this here valise, mister, I guess you must be this D. W. H.—ain't that right?"

"I am," replied Harrigan, his jaw clenched in anger at the man's derision.

The gunman snickered, "And you're a holy reverend?"

Harrigan answered softly, "I am a minister of the Gospel."

The rest of the passengers were clearly stunned by this revelation. They had all assumed he was a gambler of some sort; he had certainly never hinted that he was a man of God.

Waving the Bible at his friends, the leader of the gunmen guffawed, "Hey, fellas, we got us a Bible thumper here! Maybe we ought to sing a few hymns and let him preach to us!"

Del Harrigan's dark blue eyes grew cold. "Put the Bible back in the valise," he said with quiet authority.

Shaking his head with an insolent grin, the man replied, "Well now, boys, did you hear that? He talks awful tough for a parson."

While the three men were mocking Del Harrigan, Mack Wheeler made a desperate move. Lunging quickly, he grabbed for the leader's revolver, trying to wrest it from his hand. The Bible fell to the ground as the gunman fought to keep his grip on his weapon.

Everyone's attention turned to the struggle over the gun. Seeing his chance, Harrigan dashed toward the gunman standing closest to him and with swift precision chopped him on the back of the neck with an open hand. As the man went down, unconscious, Harrigan grabbed his weapon and got the drop on the second man before he could even bring his rifle up. With a look of disgust on his face, he obeyed Harrigan's order and dropped his weapon in the dust.

At the same moment, the revolver Mack Wheeler and the leader were grappling over discharged, sending the slug harmlessly toward the sky. While keeping a steady eye on the second gunman, Harrigan shouted at the leader, "That's enough!"

Seeing that he and his men had been bested, the man

quit struggling and released the weapon into Mack Wheeler's hands.

Harrigan held the rifle at the ready and told the other passengers, "Collect their guns, gentlemen, and make sure they're not carrying any concealed derringers or knives. Then go through their saddlebags. I don't want them left with any weapons they might be able to use against us."

"You can't do that, Reverend!" complained the leader. "This is Sioux country! A white man ain't got a chance against them redskins if he ain't armed!"

"I guess you'll have to hightail it back to civilization right pronto then, won't you?" Harrigan responded dryly. "I'd be a complete fool if I let you keep your guns—and I pride myself on *not* being a fool."

When the guns were all gathered, Harrigan instructed the men to put them inside the stagecoach. The driver jumped down from the box and picked up his gun as well as his shotgunner's, looking at Harrigan with admiration. "That was some fancy work you did there, Mist—uh, I mean, Reverend Harrigan." He scratched his head in bewilderment, adding, "I'll be danged. I never would've figured you for a preacher."

Harrigan grinned. "Nor would a lot of other people." Handing the rifle to the driver, he walked over to where his Bible lay and picked it up, dusting it off. He examined it carefully and was pleased to see that none of the pages had ripped. Satisfied, he placed it back in the valise and snapped the lid shut.

After putting the valise inside the coach, Harrigan strode over to the two gunmen and ordered, "Pick up your friend over there and throw him on his horse. And you'd better ride east when you mount up. If you follow us, I'll see to it that you regret that decision. You hear me?"

The leader's eyes narrowed in anger. Then he mumbled, "I never seen a preacherman like you. I thought reverends were supposed to be meek—you know, like Jesus."

Harrigan laughed humorlessly. "I guess a lot of folks

have the same mistaken idea, mister. Meek does not mean weak." Standing erect, the former officer pointed toward the gunmen's horses and commanded, "Now mount up and ride!"

The passengers and crew watched as the two men dragged their unconscious cohort over to his horse and draped him over the saddle. Then they climbed onto their horses and spurred them away. Assured that the scoundrels would give them no further trouble, Harrigan wheeled about and gestured toward the coach. "Let's get on our way, folks. I'm more anxious than ever to get this journey over with."

Everyone scampered aboard, and the driver snapped the reins with a flourish, setting the team in motion.

The gunmen had reined in their horses a little way off, giving their unconscious friend a chance to recover. Looking back over his shoulder at the bobbing stagecoach, barely visible through a dust cloud, the leader of the trio felt his gorge rising along with his anger.

The injured man began to moan, and the leader asked him, "You gonna be all right, Earl?"

Shaking his head slowly to clear it, the man mumbled, "Yeah. Just give me a few more minutes."

The third man inquired, "We gonna get some more guns and go after Wheeler again, Duke?"

The leader pounded his fist into his palm. "You've got my solemn vow on that, friend. Only this time Mack Wheeler dies—along with that bullnecked preacher!"

Chapter Seven

As the stagecoach continued westward, Mack Wheeler sat silently staring out the window, unable to look his fellow passengers in the eye. Communicating wordlessly with each other, the other travelers privately decided that Wheeler was either too embarrassed or still too frightened to speak.

Albert Bittner pulled his gaze away from Wheeler and looked at Del Harrigan, smiling crookedly and shaking his head with bemusement. "I'm sure I don't have to tell you, Reverend Harrigan, that Linna and I were awfully surprised to hear you're a preacher."

Del Harrigan smiled. "You mean because I don't dress in a long-tailed black coat and walk around with a solemn expression on my face?"

"Well . . . uh, yes, I guess so. I have to confess we were sure you were a gambler because of the way you dress, what with your pinstriped suit and the fancy Stetson and boots and all." He paused, adding, "I guess what they say about not judging a book by its cover is true. But you just don't fit the mold."

Harrigan chuckled and then confessed, "I've always been one to make my own mold, Mr. Bittner."

Linna Bittner spoke up, asking, "Would you mind telling us why you chose to be a preacher?"

"Not at all," Harrigan replied, leaning back in his seat. "You see, I had seen so much dying and suffering for all those years during the Civil War that when it was finally over, I wanted more than anything to serve God and my fellow man. I thought long and hard about how I could best do that, and I finally enrolled in the seminary in Philadelphia. That was in the spring of sixty-seven. When I graduated in 1871, I took over a small church in Lancaster. I don't mean this as a boast, but the congregation grew quite a bit under my leadership."

"How very commendable," Linna told him sincerely.

Harrigan smiled. "Thank you. At any rate, during the first year of my ministry there, I married my childhood sweetheart. Her name was Mary." He paused and looked down. "Just three years later, Mary died giving birth to our first child. The baby died too."

"Oh, I'm so sorry," Linna exclaimed. "That must have been terribly difficult for you."

"It was," he agreed softly. "I tried to continue as pastor of the Lancaster church, but everything there reminded me of my wife. It was simply too painful, and I finally realized that I needed to go somewhere else and begin a new life."

"And that new life will be in Red Buffalo?" Linna asked. "You've accepted a pastorate there?"

"Yes, ma'am. The Red Buffalo Community Church. A few months ago, I learned through a fellow minister that a preacher I had known as a youth—a man who's been pastor of the Red Buffalo church for a number of years—is about to retire. I wrote to him and asked if he would recommend me to his congregation. He did, and they chose me to be their new pastor on Reverend Burke's endorsement."

Neal Jones, dabbing at his sweaty face with a handkerchief, interrupted. "I don't mean this as an insult, Reverend Harrigan, but you just flat don't look or behave like a preacher. I mean, I can't imagine a preacher acting the way you did back there with those men."

Harrigan grinned. "I realize that most people have an image fixed in their minds of what a preacher should be like—a frail little man with spectacles slipping down his nose who wouldn't swat a fly."

Jones laughed. "You certainly read *my* mind."

"Do you know your Bible at all, Mr. Jones?"

"Well, a little bit . . . but not much," he admitted.

"Perhaps you recall Elijah—he was no pushover. Nor were John the Baptist or Peter and Paul. There's certainly ample precedent sprinkled throughout the Bible for tough-minded and tough-bodied preachers." Harrigan laughed, adding, "Not, mind you, that I'm comparing myself to any of those fellas."

"Well, you've sure made a believer out of me," Jones told him.

"I'd say that goes for the rest of us, too," Albert Bittner chuckled.

The passengers fell silent again, lost in their own reveries. Harrigan looked across at Mack Wheeler, detecting a film of tears in the man's eyes. Reaching over and laying a hand on his shoulder, the preacher asked, "Mr. Wheeler, is there anything I can do to help?"

Wheeler's head came slowly around, and he seemed reluctant to meet Harrigan's gaze. Finally he looked at him directly and replied, "I . . . I don't know. It's like I've got a great big dam inside me and it's about to break." He sighed. "Maybe if I tell you all about it, it'll ease the pressure."

"I'm ready to listen," Harrigan assured him softly. "That is if you don't mind these other folks hearing it, too."

Wheeler, his eyes desperate and frightened, looked over the faces of the others. "No, I don't mind."

Harrigan sat back in his seat and mopped the sweat from his face. Then he declared with an encouraging smile, "I'm listening."

Mack Wheeler stared out the window again, as if not seeing the faces of the others made it easier for him to tell his tale. After some hesitation, he started talking about his wonderful and beautiful wife, Ginny, confessing that he had mistreated her almost from the beginning of their marriage. He left out none of the sordid details of his gambling problems and his affairs with other women.

"I take it your wife decided she had had enough and asked you to leave," Harrigan interjected when Wheeler paused to regain his composure.

Shaking his head sadly, Wheeler confessed, "Quite the opposite. She forgave me more times than any man deserved. No, I deserted her some six months ago when I ran off to Sioux City with a cheap saloon woman." He looked down at his lap, saying ashamedly, "I left a note for Ginny when I ran away, telling her that I would send her divorce papers. But . . . but I just never was able to make myself get the divorce. I suppose I finally realize that I've been a complete fool and I really love her. Although I told myself that the reason I was going home was to sell our house to get the money to pay off Perry Prince, I guess the fact is that I want to make an attempt to reconcile with my wife—that is, if she'll have me."

Del Harrigan leaned across the aisle and put a comforting hand on Wheeler's shoulder again. "Frankly, it might not be easy to get her to listen to you, since you have indeed treated her very badly. But if you *can* get her to listen, once she hears what you have to say, I'm sure she'll realize how sincere you are. And I want you to know that I would be pleased to offer you counsel if Mrs. Wheeler is willing."

Mack Wheeler looked into Harrigan's eyes. Smiling tentatively, he said softly, "I really appreciate that. And you'll be in a good position because Ginny's a member of the church you'll be pastoring." A cloud suddenly passed over his face and his eyes became fearful. "But then again," he gloomily announced, "what good would it do me to get my wife back if I'll be dead?"

"You're talking about Mr. Prince sending more men after you?"

"Yes."

"My advice is to send a letter to him immediately and tell him you sincerely intend to honor your debt. Enclose a token payment with the letter and ask to arrange a mutually satisfactory time period over which you will pay

71

everything back. Above all, ask for leniency." Harrigan shrugged. "It'd be worth a try."

"Yeah," agreed Wheeler, "you're right. That's what I'll do. If I can just get Ginny back, I know everything else will work out." He smiled, and for the first time a look of optimism lit up Mack Wheeler's round face.

The stagecoach started slowing down as it swerved off the road toward a lonely swing station. When the vehicle came to a halt in a cloud of dust, the passengers alighted to refresh themselves while the horses were switched.

Returning to the stage, the passengers found the driver and shotgunner bending over the left rear wheel. The driver was tapping the wheel housing with the tips of his fingers, and he looked up to explain, "There's gonna be a slight delay, folks. This wheel's gone dry and it's real hot. We'll have to let it cool down some, then repack it with grease. It'll take about an hour."

The passengers had no objections to having more time to stretch their legs and find some shade. They all gathered together under an enormous cottonwood near the station building, waiting patiently for the work to be completed. A little less than an hour later, the driver came walking toward them while wiping his hands with an old rag. "Okay, folks," he announced, "we're all set and ready to go now."

With a collective sigh, the passengers picked themselves up and headed for the stage, where the shotgunner was already sitting up on the driver's box. The Bittners entered the coach first while the driver climbed up to his seat. Then Neal Jones and Wesley Sartin followed, with Mack Wheeler and Del Harrigan waiting their turns.

From the corner of his eye, Harrigan caught a glint of sunlight on metal, the only warning before two rifles suddenly cracked almost simultaneously. As a bullet buzzed past his own head like an angry hornet and chewed into the coach, Harrigan heard Wheeler grunt before falling into a heap on the ground, a crimson stain spreading in the middle of his shirt. Inside the coach, Linna Bittner screamed.

Harrigan dropped to the ground beside the motion-less Mack Wheeler. Glancing quickly in the direction of the shots, he saw one man astride a horse and two more leaping into their saddles from the knee-high tawny grass. Although he caught just a glimpse of them, the preacher recognized Perry Prince's henchmen.

Shouting up to the driver, who was having a hard time controlling the frightened horses, Harrigan told him to throw down his rifle. He caught the weapon and at the same time called in to the other passengers, "See what you can do for Mr. Wheeler!"

In motion even as he spoke, the preacher whirled about and shouldered the rifle. Two of the attackers were already galloping away eastward, while the third man was lagging somewhat. He was about to leap onto his horse when Harrigan took aim and shouted, "Drop it!"

The man spun around, worked the lever of his weapon, and shot from the hip, but the bullet plowed harmlessly into the dirt ten feet away from Harrigan.

"Drop it or I'll shoot!" the preacher bellowed.

The attacker only worked the rifle's lever again.

Harrigan had no choice, and as the man was bringing the rifle into play, he squeezed the trigger. The man took the slug in his chest and fell into the tall grass. Even though he knew it was useless, Harrigan sent a shot after the two retreating men. But they were beyond the rifle's range, and they galloped safely away.

Harrigan thought briefly about jumping on the gun-man's horse and pursuing Prince's men, but he knew they had too much of a head start. He would never catch them. Frustrated and angry, he turned and looked down at Mack Wheeler and then at the faces of the others, who, along with the stationmaster, were all gathered around Wheel-er's still form. He was obviously dead.

The preacher knelt beside the body and gently closed the sightless eyes. Then he stood up and levered another cartridge into the chamber of his rifle, moving cautiously toward the spot where the gunman had fallen. Harrigan found him and saw that, like Mack Wheeler, he had taken the slug directly in the heart.

Harrigan hefted the corpse into his arms and, walking to the man's horse, draped the body over the saddle. Then he led the horse across the road to the stationmaster, asking, "Would you mind burying him? At least you'll get a pretty good-looking horse for your trouble."

The stationmaster assessed the horse and then looked back at Harrigan and agreed: "Seems a fair trade." Taking the reins, he led the horse bearing the dead gunman to the nearby barn.

Harrigan stood over Mack Wheeler's lifeless form and said to the driver, "Billy, I guess we ought to wrap him in a blanket or a tarp and take him home to his wife." He sighed deeply, adding softly, "It sure isn't the kind of reunion he was hoping for. . . ."

It was just before noon the following day when Frank Meeker looked out the window of the Butterfield office in Red Buffalo as the stage pulled in. It was Saturday, and many people were milling about on the street, busy doing their weekly chores. Hurrying out the door, Meeker stood on the boardwalk waiting for the stage to come to a complete stop. When it did, he hopped down off the boardwalk and stepped to the door of the stage, pulling it open.

"Welcome to Red Buffalo, folks. My name is Frank Meeker. I'm the agent here." He looked up at the driver, asking, "Need a hand getting some of that baggage down, Billy?"

"Nope, we can handle it—but as a matter of fact, we've got somethin' here that needs some special handlin', I'm afraid." Gesturing to the rear of the luggage rack, the driver indicated Mack Wheeler's blanket-wrapped corpse.

Meeker's gaze followed Billy Bartlett's thumb. Looking back at the driver, he asked, "Is that a body?"

"Yep," confirmed the driver with a nod, climbing down. "I'm sure you know him. Name was Mack Wheeler."

The agent's mouth dropped open. "Mack Wheeler?"

"That's right. He boarded the stage in Sioux City,

74

lookin' like a scared rabbit. The folks he was runnin' from caught up to us and killed him yesterday. Reverend Harrigan will fill you in on it."

Frank Meeker felt his heart pounding, and he realized he was having a hard time keeping a smile off his face. Now that Mack Wheeler was dead, Ginny was no longer shackled to him, and she was free to marry again. He abruptly shook such thoughts from his mind to focus on the business at hand, and while the driver and the shotgunner were lowering Wheeler's corpse to the boardwalk, Meeker scanned the faces of the passengers who stood beside him, waiting for their luggage. He wanted to be the first to welcome the new pastor to Red Buffalo.

Looking past the tall man whom he assumed to be a gambler, he peered carefully at Neal Jones and Wesley Sartin. He quickly eliminated them because they both seemed to be somewhere in their fifties—considerably older than he believed the new pastor to be. The man with the young wife was about the right age, but Reverend Burke had told the congregation that Harrigan was not married. Walking back to the coach, Meeker stuck his head inside. Puzzled, he looked over at the driver. "I can't seem to find Reverend Harrigan. You *did* say he was on the coach."

"Yeah," replied the driver. "That's him standin' right there behind you."

Meeker spun around and looked at the tall, handsome, well-dressed man. His eyes widened. "This is—?"

"I'm Del Harrigan, Mr. Meeker," confirmed the preacher, extending his hand.

Meeker met Harrigan's grip and then smiled and said, "You'll have to forgive me, Preacher. I . . . I wasn't expecting—"

"No one ever is," cut in Harrigan, grinning. Then his face sobered, and he asked, "Can you get your undertaker over here quick? It might be best to let him have the body immediately. Mr. Wheeler was killed yesterday."

"Oh . . . sure, I understand," replied Meeker. "I'll send someone to get him."

Frank Meeker was almost ashamed of himself. Far from feeling no sorrow whatsoever for Mack Wheeler, there was only relief . . . sweet relief that Ginny's no-good husband was dead and out of the way. Calling over a young boy who stood gawking at the corpse, he sent the lad to fetch the undertaker. Then he helped the shotgunner lower Del Harrigan's trunk to the ground.

Harrigan carried his trunk into the stage office, explaining to Meeker that he would come for it as soon as he knew where he would be staying. Then he asked, "Can you direct me to Reverend Burke's home? I feel that he and I should both go and break the news to Mrs. Wheeler that her husband is dead."

"I'll do better than that, Preacher," Meeker answered. "I'll take you there myself. Besides, I think I should go along with you to be with Ginny when she receives the news. She and I are very good friends."

"Fine. Can we go right away?"

"Just let me get this stage back on the road, and we'll go," replied Meeker.

Del Harrigan bade the other passengers good-bye, wishing them a safe journey, and stood waving as the stage pulled away.

Frank Meeker turned to the preacher. "Okay. Let's go."

During the ten-minute walk to Cletus Burke's house, Del Harrigan looked carefully around and liked what he saw. While the commercial district was not large, what stores and shops there were seemed to be thriving, and the homes in the residential district were well cared for. In fact, the entire town bespoke the citizens' pride.

When they reached the old pastor's house, Del Harrigan greeted his old friend warmly. Susan Burke cordially showed Harrigan and Meeker into the parlor, offering tea, but Harrigan declined, saying, "I'm afraid our socializing will have to wait. We have more pressing matters to attend to." He then gave the Burkes the news about Mack Wheeler's violent death and explained why the errant husband had been returning to Red Buffalo.

The three men quickly set out for Ginny Wheeler's home, and a few minutes later they stepped onto the porch of the small, neat white house and knocked on the door. Hasty footsteps sounded from inside and the door opened. Del Harrigan was immediately taken with the stunning beauty of Ginny Wheeler, and her sweet smile when she greeted her old pastor warmed his heart. A puzzled expression lingered on her face as she looked at the three men on her doorstep. She turned to Reverend Burke questioningly.

When the pastor introduced Del Harrigan, her face momentarily betrayed her surprise, but she quickly recovered and extended her hand, declaring warmly, "Welcome to Red Buffalo, Reverend Harrigan."

"Thank you, Mrs. Wheeler, it's a pleasure to be here." Looking at her perhaps a bit more closely than he had intended, Del Harrigan could see in Ginny's lovely brown eyes that she had been deeply hurt and scarred.

Ginny invited the three men into the house, directed them to chairs in the parlor, and took a seat herself. Reverend Burke spoke to her gently. "Ginny, I'm afraid this isn't a social call. In fact, we have some rather bad news to give you." He paused and cleared his throat. "Your husband is dead."

She was briefly taken aback, but almost immediately composed herself. "I see," she said simply.

Closely observing Ginny's reaction, Harrigan thought it was quite apparent that the young widow had long ago lost all love for Mack Wheeler. He assumed that Wheeler's continual abuse of her affections had killed any love she had felt for him.

Ginny sighed and then asked, "How did Mack die?"

Harrigan gave her all the details—of Wheeler's having boarded the stage in fear, his admission that he had mistreated her but had hoped they could reconcile, and how Perry Prince's men had followed the stage and shot her husband to death. In closing, Harrigan told her that the body had been taken to the funeral parlor.

Ginny turned to her old minister and softly told him, "Pastor Burke, I'm truly sorry that Mack had to die such a violent death, but I have no feeling left inside me for him. May I ask you to see to it that Mack is buried quickly and without ceremony? I will attend, of course—but I want no other mourners there—and I'll pay the undertaker for his services."

Burke nodded his assent and stood up to leave. The other two men rose as well, but Frank Meeker moved to Ginny's side and took her hand, saying, "I'll stay here with you, my dear. You need comforting, I'm sure. I know this has upset you."

Ginny gently but firmly pulled her hand free. She was equally firm when she rebuffed his offer, telling him, "I really don't need any comfort, Frank, thank you. As far as I'm concerned, my husband has been dead for a long time."

Walking the three men to the door, the young widow thanked them for their kindness. As Harrigan stepped onto the porch, she smiled and extended her hand to him again, telling him, "Although we shall all miss Reverend Burke, it's comforting to know that he has found such an able replacement."

After bidding farewell to Frank Meeker at the corner, the two preachers returned to Cletus Burke's home to discuss church business. Harrigan learned that the church had been meeting in the town hall ever since its inception. The congregation had finally accumulated enough money in the church coffers to purchase some land at the south end of town near the schoolhouse, leaving them with fifteen hundred dollars toward the construction of a new building. Cletus Burke had determined that with the men of the congregation doing the work, an ample facility could be built for three thousand dollars, and when Harrigan took over, his foremost priority would be to raise the necessary balance.

Reverend Burke told the younger minister he would resign officially at the service the following morning, at which time Harrigan would be installed as pastor.

"Tell me, Cletus, where will I be living?"

"Well, my boy, lodgings will be provided for you at the Red Buffalo Hotel—which, of course, will be paid for by the ministry until the new church and parsonage can be built."

Nodding, Harrigan responded, "That will do fine for the time being, although I certainly hope we'll be able to begin construction as soon as possible." The young preacher looked at the old-timer curiously and then asked, "By the way, how did the town come by the name Red Buffalo? It's most unusual, isn't it—even out here in the West?"

Laughing, Burke agreed, "That it is. Actually, it was once called Dakota City, but the name was changed after a devastating prairie fire in the summer of sixty-seven. The entire town burned to the ground and the people gallantly started all over, scraping and scratching to rebuild. When the new town was finally completed, the citizens decided they should call it Red Buffalo because that's the Sioux name for a prairie fire."

"Oh? Why is that?"

"Well, you see, when they're driven across the plains by the wind, the roaring flames sound exactly like a buffalo stampede. And the people felt that since the town had been destroyed by the Red Buffalo, they would pay homage, in a sense, by so naming it." The old man raised his eyebrows, adding, "It seems to have worked all these years. We haven't had a prairie fire since."

Chapter Eight

The town hall was completely filled as the entire congregation of the Red Buffalo Community Church attended the Sunday service that marked the official retirement of Reverend Cletus Burke and the installation of Reverend Delbert Wade Harrigan. That afternoon the parishioners held a picnic by the river just outside of town to welcome their new pastor, and at its conclusion, Ginny Wheeler and another young widow, Shirley Taylor, approached Harrigan and invited him for supper the next evening. The preacher accepted the invitation, saying that six o'clock would be fine. Then he touched his hat brim and left.

Standing nearby, Frank Meeker had watched the threesome talking animatedly and felt his anger rising. *Why did the congregation have to choose such a tall, handsome, and eligible replacement?* he asked himself. He heard the two women extend the invitation to Harrigan, and as soon as the preacher left, he walked over and tried his best to be included in the offer—to no avail. Meeker was extremely perturbed that he was not invited, but he knew there was nothing he could do about it. He tried to mask his disappointment when Ginny and Shirley politely told him good-bye and walked away together as he stood watching glumly.

Del Harrigan spent most of Monday strolling around Red Buffalo, introducing himself to the townspeople. Though many of them were not in his congregation, he wanted to meet them and let them know that anyone was welcome to call on him at any time.

One of the calls Harrigan made was at the office of the town marshal. When the preacher's tall, muscular form filled the doorway, the young lawman, seated at his desk, looked up and smiled. Laying down the pen in his hand, the young man rose to his feet and extended his hand.

"Good morning to you, sir," he declared expansively. "I don't have to ask who you are."

"Oh?" Harrigan responded.

"No, indeed. You're the talk of the town, Reverend Harrigan. If I've heard your description once, I've heard it two dozen times."

"I don't have to ask who you are, either," countered Harrigan, grinning, "since the badge on your vest tells me you must be Marshal Teal Peck."

Looking closely at Peck as they shook hands, Harrigan was surprised at the lawman's extreme youth. He was sure Peck had not yet reached twenty-five. "Just wanted to stop in and get acquainted, Marshal," Harrigan told him, pushing his hat to the back of his head. "I must confess, I didn't expect to find a man so young."

"You wouldn't have if you'd come six weeks sooner," replied Peck sadly. "My father was marshal of Red Buffalo, and I was his deputy. He was killed at the end of May by a wild bunch of buffalo hunters. They came to town to have a good time and got too rowdy."

Harrigan shook his head in sympathy. "I'm so sorry. I'm sure your father was a fine man. I've heard about your buffalo hunters out here, and I understand they can be pretty ornery if they have a mind to be."

"That's right. Buffalo hunters are to this area what trail hands are to the Kansas cow towns. Whenever they show up, there's sure to be trouble."

"Well, Marshal," the preacher declared, "if you ever need a helping hand when the buffalo hunters or anyone else stirs up trouble, I want you to know you can feel free to call on me."

81

Teal Peck looked at Harrigan in bewilderment and then thanked him for the offer.

That evening the new parson knocked on Ginny Wheeler's door. Ginny opened it, and Del Harrigan's heart began to pound at the sight of the breathtakingly beautiful young widow. Her hair done up, with tiny curls ringing her forehead, she was dressed in a cream-colored skirt and a frilly white blouse that was edged with lace at the collar and cuffs.

Greeting him with a smile, she ushered him into the house. Harrigan looked around and then cleared his slightly constricted throat and told her, "You have a lovely home, Mrs. Wheeler."

"Thank you," replied Ginny. Moving toward the rear of the house, she said, "Come out to the kitchen with me. We can talk while I finish preparing supper."

Following on her heels, the preacher's mouth began to water as the smell of cooking food reached his nostrils. They reached the kitchen and he looked around, surprised that they were alone. "Isn't Mrs. Taylor here?"

"No, she isn't," Ginny answered, moving to the counter where she began cutting a loaf of still-hot bread. Gesturing toward a chair, she invited him to sit down and continued, "Shirley sent her young nephew over about an hour ago to tell me that she was feeling slightly ill, so she thought it best not to join us."

"I'm sorry to hear that," responded the preacher. "Will she need any medical attention?"

"Apparently not. Her nephew said her ailment was quite minor." Ginny set the plate of hot bread in front of the preacher and then opened the oven door, letting the smell of baked chicken waft through the room. Over her shoulder, she said, "I hope you like chicken."

Harrigan smiled. "Yes, ma'am. But only if it's not foul."

Ginny laughed, and from the look in her eyes it was apparent that she liked this tall, handsome man.

When all the food was on the table, she sat down

across from Harrigan and asked him to say grace. When they began eating, the preacher thought to himself he had not tasted such wonderful food since Mary had died, and while he devoured the food, he was also devouring Ginny's captivating face with his eyes.

Talking easily, they discussed many subjects, and the conversation eventually turned to their backgrounds. Ginny told him of her childhood and then of her marriage to Mack Wheeler and the heartaches that followed. Speaking more cheerfully, she said, "But I've found great fulfillment in my teaching. The children are such a delight." She paused a moment and then queried, "Do you like children, Pastor?"

"I do, indeed," he replied quickly. "As they say, I used to be one myself."

Again Ginny was struck by Harrigan's humor. She laughed and said, "Maybe I should ask if you like schoolteachers."

The preacher chuckled. "Well, I remember one old crabapple I thoroughly detested. Had her from first grade through the fifth. But my sixth grade year, a new teacher came to my school, and she was real nice—and quite pretty, too." He smiled warmly at her. "I had one of those schoolboy crushes on her that I'll bet your boys have on you."

Ginny's face colored, and she quickly steered the subject away from herself.

The preacher sensed that the young widow felt as he did—that each found in the other a kindred spirit. Del Harrigan was aware of a fire kindling in his heart, a fire that had been sparked quite suddenly by this wonderful young woman, and he knew if he let it happen, he could easily fall in love with her. He had to resist the urge to reach over and take her hand to comfort her, for the pain she had experienced because of her husband was quite evident in her expressive brown eyes. She had made it quite clear that not only had she been repeatedly hurt by Mack, but that she had been starved for love. Harrigan told himself that if she belonged to him, she would never lack for love.

When the meal was over, Harrigan helped Ginny do the dishes, and then they moved out to the front porch to enjoy the cool evening breeze. They chatted for another half hour. Then the handsome minister bade the young widow good night, and Ginny went back into the house.

Going to her bedroom, Ginny Wheeler lit the lamp on her dresser and sat down on the edge of her bed. She pondered the feelings that were stirring in her heart, troubled by their intensity. Standing up, she paced slowly back and forth in the room, telling herself that it would be a long time before she could ever fall in love again. Her image in the dresser mirror caught her eye, and she stopped and stared at herself. "Besides, Ginny Wheeler," she admonished her reflection, "you could never be good enough to be the wife of a man of God."

At that moment there was a knock at Ginny's door, and her heart quickened pace. Perhaps Del Harrigan had forgotten something. She found herself almost running to the front of the house and forced her legs to slow to a mere walk. Halting by the door, Ginny smoothed the hair at the nape of her neck and composed her face. When she turned the knob and pulled the door open, she felt a keen sense of disappointment at the sight of Frank Meeker. Peering at him by the lamplight that spilled out the door, she saw that his face was filled with anger.

Without waiting for her to speak, Meeker blurted, "Pretty chummy with the preacher, aren't you?"

Ginny's mouth flew open and she could feel the color flooding her face. "Whatever do you mean by that, Frank?"

Meeker's voice was sullen. "I thought Shirley Taylor was supposed to be here. Well, I've been watching long enough to know that you and Harrigan were in this house alone!"

Ginny folded her arms across her chest. Regarding Meeker with cold eyes, she fumed, "For your information, Shirley fell ill and couldn't come. Reverend Harrigan and I did not plan to dine by ourselves."

"Well, then, you should have called off th—"

"Don't you tell me what I should have done!" she stormed, cutting off his words. "How dare you come here and talk to me like this! It's none of your business who I have in this house. Do you hear me? And how dare you spy on me! Where were you? Hiding in the bushes? What unmitigated gall!"

"But, Ginny, I—"

"Get off my porch!" she snapped, as she slammed the door. Still fuming, she turned down the lamp and went to bed.

Early the next morning, the Reverend Del Harrigan went to the Red Buffalo Corral and Stable and purchased a good horse. Then he set out to tour the area. There was a vast difference between this land and the densely wooded hills of Pennsylvania where he had been brought up. Here, a person could see for miles, for though the prairie was thick with tall grass, there were few trees. Only along creeks and rivers was there sufficient moisture to support thick stands of them.

As he rode through the grassland, the preacher looked with delight at the lavender and gold wildflowers moving in the breeze amid the brown grass. That was something that Del Harrigan had noticed right away about this vast prairie—there was always a breeze, if not a downright brisk wind. The air never seemed to be motionless, day or night.

After a two-hour ride, he went back into town and stopped at the site owned by the church. While he was looking it over, his eyes shifted to the nearby schoolhouse, and he thought of Ginny Wheeler. He realized that, in more ways than one, he was excited and optimistic about his future in Red Buffalo.

Looking again at the building site, Harrigan decided on a plan to raise the additional money so they could proceed with the construction. He had some inheritance money in a Philadelphia bank, and he decided that he would donate a thousand dollars to the building fund and then ask the church members to dig down deep and come up with the remaining five hundred. Feeling content, he clucked to his horse and headed back to the stable.

It was shortly after sunrise the following morning when Del Harrigan was awakened by a knock at the door. Slipping his pants on, he opened the door and found himself looking into the harried face of a teenage boy who looked vaguely familiar.

Holding his hat in his hand, the youth said, "Reverend Harrigan, my name is Eric Standish. Me and my grandparents, we're members of your congregation, and I live with them on their farm about six miles northwest of town. My grandpa, he's real sick, and Doc Curtin says he don't know how much longer he's got. Grandpa knows he's dyin', and he asked me to come and see if you'd come back to the farm with me. Will you?"

"Of course, son," Harrigan assured him, recognizing the boy as one of the people he had seen but not spoken with at the church picnic. "Come in while I get dressed, and tell me everything."

While the preacher donned his shirt and pulled on his boots, Eric Standish explained that his grandfather had been mean and wicked all his life. Now that he was about to depart this life, he was afraid to die without a preacher to help him find peace.

"I'm glad you came for me. It's never too late to make peace with God," Harrigan told the youth. He put a comforting hand on Eric's shoulder as he guided him out of the room.

It was late morning by the time Del Harrigan left the Standish farm and headed back for Red Buffalo. He had ridden barely a mile when his eye caught movement on the prairie some five hundred yards ahead. He rode to a crest from where he could make out five riderless horses in a cluster, two of them black-and-white pintos. As he rode closer, he could see that three men had another man on the ground, and they were beating him mercilessly. Two small children stood watching, their hands to their mouths as if in fear.

Harrigan spurred his horse into a gallop. As he drew closer, he could see that the children were Indians, a boy and a girl, as was the man being kicked and pummeled. Thundering up to the scene, the preacher bellowed, "Hey! Stop that right now!"

Reining in, he leaped out of the saddle before his horse had even stopped. The three men looked up from what they were doing, and Harrigan recognized them as citizens of Red Buffalo. The old man they were beating—a Sioux, gray and wrinkled—lay on the ground moaning in pain.

Hurrying to the attackers, Harrigan demanded, "What's going on here?"

The three townsmen stood up, and there was a mixture of hatred and anger on their faces as they glared at Harrigan. The tallest one eyed the intruder sharply and then grunted, "We're just teachin' this Sioux scum a lesson. What's it to you, Reverend?"

Stepping closer, Harrigan growled, "Seems to me things are a little lopsided here, what with three of you against one old man. Now just leave him alone. The lesson is over."

The big one looked at his friends and grinned. "Maybe the holy man needs a lesson himself, huh, boys?"

Harrigan did not flinch. Instead, staring at the man, he pointed to the Indian and ordered, "Help him up."

An insolent snarl curled the man's lip. "I ain't touchin' no dirty red man unless it's with my boot or my fist."

The smallest of the three men scowled at the preacher and blurted, "Why don't you just go tend to your church business?"

"Yeah," grunted the third man. "Vamoose right now, or you'll be layin' right next to the stinkin' Sioux. We ain't through teachin' him that lesson, and if you try to butt in, you'll be right sorry."

Fire ignited inside Harrigan's veins, and he reacted

instantly. Lashing out with his right foot, he kicked the biggest man in the groin. When the man doubled over, falling to the ground, the preacher focused on the little man standing next to him. He boxed him hard on the ear and sent him reeling. Pivoting, Harrigan saw the remaining man clawing for the revolver on his hip, swearing loudly. The preacher's foot shot out again, kicking the gun from the man's hand. Shock registered in the man's bulging eyes as Harrigan sprang at him, knocking him out with a hard punch to the jaw.

The biggest man was growling like a wounded buffalo and filling the air with profanity as he rose to his feet, reaching for his gun. But Harrigan was too fast as he leaped and drove a hard fist into the man's soft belly. Then he took one step back and slammed him with a powerful blow to the jaw. The man crumpled and fell unconscious at the feet of the Sioux children, who quickly jumped aside in fright.

At that instant Harrigan caught a hissing sound from behind, and he dodged just as the little man swung the butt of a revolver at his head. Before the little man could regain his balance, Harrigan smashed a fist into his jaw, and he slumped to the ground and lay still.

Collecting their guns, Harrigan threw them as far as he could into the tall grass. Then he went over to the frightened children and, kneeling in front of them, told them softly, "You don't have to be afraid now. Nobody is going to hurt you."

Though they did not understand his words, his tone was obviously enough to reassure them, for they both smiled weakly.

Harrigan then knelt beside the old Indian, who was grimacing with pain. "Do you understand English, old fella?" he asked gently.

"Yes," the ancient Sioux replied, his body doubled up into a fetal position.

"Let me take a look here and see how bad you're hurt." A brief examination revealed that the old man's back was severely bruised, his ribs were probably cracked, and his face was cut.

Harrigan introduced himself to the Indian and told him, "I am going to take you into town to our doctor. You need medical attention." He looked over at the three unconscious attackers and then back at the old man, asking, "What happened here?"

The Sioux told Harrigan his name was Lone Fox and that he and his two great-grandchildren had been riding from one Sioux village to another. They had come upon the three men, who had suddenly surrounded them, dragged him from his horse, and begun beating him.

Harrigan shook his head in disgust. He suggested that Lone Fox tell the children to go on to the village and explain that the preacher was taking him into Red Buffalo to care for his wounds and that he would return to his people as soon as he could. When the children nodded their understanding, Harrigan helped them onto their pinto and they rode away.

He walked back to where the Indian lay, gently lifted him into his arms, and carefully placed him on the other pinto's back, making sure he was secure. While he was doing so, the three men came to, and Harrigan watched them stagger around looking for their guns. The preacher called to the trio, and when they looked over at him, their eyes were filled with hate.

"I want to know why you were beating up that defenseless old man," Harrigan demanded.

The biggest one narrowed his eyes and muttered, "We don't like what his people did to Custer and the Seventh Cavalry."

Harrigan's voice was cold and steady. "And so you took your revenge out on a feeble old man who had nothing to do with what happened to Custer." He looked at them with contempt. "You men are complete fools. Custer brought the massacre on himself. He'd still be alive today if he'd followed orders the way a soldier is supposed to."

The three men swore savagely at the preacher, calling

him a traitor and an Indian lover, but Harrigan ignored them. He mounted his horse and, holding tightly to the pinto's reins, led the pony toward town. Looking back at Lone Fox, he saw that despite the old man's obvious pain, he was smiling to himself.

Chapter Nine

Dr. Jesse Curtin, a small man in his late fifties, brushed back the thick shock of disheveled salt-and-pepper hair that perpetually dangled over his forehead. With careful, experienced hands, he stood over the examining table and assessed the damage that had been done to the old Sioux Indian. While the physician probed, he spoke over his shoulder to Reverend Del Harrigan, who was sitting in a chair a few feet away.

"They really worked this old man over, Pastor. He's definitely got three cracked ribs, and I'll have to put some stitches in his face, too. But his back took the worst of the injuries."

"What did they do to him, Doc?" asked Harrigan.

"Two discs in his spinal column have been crushed— and at his age, they're going to take a long time to heal. I'll have him walking again, but he'll need to stay right here in the clinic till I think he's well enough to return to his village." He looked the old man in the eyes and asked, "Do you understand what I am saying, Lone Fox?"

"Yes," responded the Indian, trying to nod. "But I have no money to pay you."

Curtin shook his head and gently smiled. "We won't worry about that." He paused and then asked, "You raise some corn out there at your village, don't you?"

"Yes."

"Tell you what. When we get you well and you're

able to do a little work again, you can pay me with a bushel of corn. How's that?"

Lone Fox smiled weakly. "It is agreed," he replied evenly.

When the physician had finished attending to the old man, he and the preacher moved Lone Fox into a bed in the recovery ward. As the two men walked back to Dr. Curtin's office, Harrigan told him, "I'll stop by tomorrow and see how he's doing." Then he added, "I suppose a message should be sent over to his village, to let his people know how long he'll have to stay in Red Buffalo."

Nodding, the doctor said, "I should have a better idea of his prognosis in another day or two. I'll keep you informed."

"Good. Well, I'd better get back to church business," Harrigan concluded, and he left the clinic.

That evening at the midweek church service, Reverend Harrigan described his building-fund plan to the parishioners, explaining that he would donate two thirds of the remaining funds that were needed for construction. Touched by his generosity, member after member of the church stood up and named a sum that they would give, and within an hour, the five-hundred-dollar balance had been pledged.

There was a spontaneous round of applause, and then Harrigan looked out over the crowd and told them, "You're a wonderful congregation, and I am very honored to be your pastor. On Sunday morning, then, we'll take our special offering at the close of the service. At that time we can all put in what we have pledged here tonight, and shortly thereafter, we can begin construction on our new buildings. Now we will conclude tonight's service by thanking the Lord for His great bounty. Let us bow our heads and—"

Suddenly there was a loud crash as the door of the town hall burst open and slammed against the wall, and everyone turned around to see what was going on. Harrigan was surprised to see the three men he had beaten earlier standing in the doorway. Fury was written all over their bruised and swollen faces.

The smallest man of the trio remained at the door, a menacing look in his eyes. He held a cocked revolver in each hand, and while his two cohorts moved up the aisle toward the pulpit, the little man barked, "Nobody move! Anyone who tries anything gets a bullet!"

Children whimpered and drew close to their mothers. The men bristled, but none of them were armed, so they dared not interfere.

As the two other toughs walked toward the lectern they drew their revolvers. The bigger man of the two scowled and muttered, "We got a mighty big score to settle with your holy man, folks—and when we're done with him, this goddamn Indian lover's gonna wish he'd stayed in goddamn Pennsylvania!"

The toughs were within ten feet of the pulpit when Harrigan boomed, "Hold it right there!" He was outraged that these men would dare barge into a church service and hold guns on his congregation.

The two men saw the look on Harrigan's face and halted.

His hands out of sight, the preacher warned the bigger man, "I've got a revolver trained on you from behind this pulpit, and I'd bet one of these slugs is just itching to find your belly! Now drop your gun—and tell your two buddies to do the same!"

The leader had his revolver aimed at the pulpit, but he had not yet cocked it. From the hesitant look on his face, it was clear that he was feeling the force of Harrigan's rage.

"I said tell them to drop their guns—and let yours hit the floor, too!"

The big tough glared at Harrigan and then hissed, "I can cut you down while you're gettin' me, holy man."

Harrigan snorted, "Maybe—but I can drill you twice while you're hunting for the hammer."

The big man forced a laugh. "Hah! You're a preacher.

93

You wouldn't shoot me—especially not right here in from of all these sweet-faced parishioners of yours."

"I'll remind them of what you said when I conduc your funeral tomorrow," came the preacher's icy rejoinder

From the back of the hall the man stationed by the door shouted, "He's bluffin', George! He ain't got no gur in there! Kill him!"

"Yeah, George," breathed the third man, who stood inches to his leader's right. "He's bluffin'! Let's take him!"

Every eye in the room was riveted on the three men at the front of the hall.

Glaring at the man named George, the preacher asked coldly, "You think I'm bluffing?"

"Sure he's bluffin', George!" his friend insisted. "Call him!"

"Shut up! It ain't your gut he's aimin' at, it's mine!" blared the tough, keeping his eyes on the man behind the pulpit. His face started to twitch from the tension, and sheen of sweat moistened his craggy brow.

The third man spoke again. "Dammit, George, I tell you he's—"

"I said shut up!" roared the thug, still not taking hi eyes off Harrigan.

"Think, man!" his cohort argued. "Why would h have a gun in the pulpit? It's nothin' but a bluff, I tell you a bluff!"

"Yeah, George!" shouted the skinny man at the rear "It don't make sense, him havin' a gun up there. Go o and blow him to the pearly gates!"

Harrigan's eyes narrowed and his jaw clenched. Fi nally he warned, "I'm getting tired of this, George. Eithe you and your partners drop your weapons, or I'm going t drop you."

Sweat dripped over the tough's eyebrows into hi eyes. Lips quivering, he grunted, "If you do, my pals wi shoot up some of your people."

"You won't be around to know *what* happens, mis ter," Harrigan challenged.

Palming sweat from his face with his free hand, the man named George mumbled, "Maybe you *are* bluffin'."

"You willing to take the chance? I'm real tired of this game." He looked intently at each man in turn. "You've got ten seconds. All three of you drop your guns, or George dies."

The tension in the room was so thick it seemed to suffocate the entire crowd. Abruptly, the leader of the trio said from the side of his mouth, "Drop your guns, boys!" and he let his weapon fall from his hand.

Del Harrigan cast an ominous glance toward the skinny man by the back door, who eased down the hammers of his revolvers and carefully laid them on the floor. The third man swore under his breath and then let his gun fall at his feet.

As the last gun clattered to the floor, a huge sigh went up from the parishioners, and they smiled at each other in relief. Some of the bolder men scrambled for the fallen weapons, holding them for safekeeping. But their preacher, immobile as a statue, kept his arm inside the pulpit and said tightly, "All right, you three, get your carcasses out of here now. Go find another place to infest."

The three men slunk out of the building, and after they had disappeared from sight, one man moved to the open door and stuck his head out, checking to make sure they had gone. Straightening, he closed the door and nodded to Harrigan, "They're gone, Preacher."

The members of Red Buffalo Community Church stared with anticipation at their minister. Had he been bluffing, or not?

A slow smile crept across Del Harrigan's mouth as he stepped away from the pulpit and raised his hands—both of them empty.

Laughter rolled through the congregation, and everyone began to cheer. Leaving their seats, the parishioners gathered around their pastor, shaking his hand and patting him on the back. One man was heard to shout above the din, "That was great, Reverend! You're my kind of preacher!"

Lingering behind after the rest of the congregation had left, Ginny Wheeler waited by the door while Harrigan moved about, snuffing out the lamps. As he approached the back of the room, he looked at her and, laughing victoriously, said, "I guess that's one church service no one will ever forget."

"You're certainly right about that," she agreed, giggling. Then her face grew serious, and she said softly, "Pastor Harrigan, I'm afraid those three troublemakers aren't through with you. Word of what happened this morning when you rescued the old Indian is already all over town, and you really shamed George Willoughby and his cronies by beating them up. I know them. You'd best keep a sharp eye over your shoulder."

"I will," he promised, moving to the last lamp and turning down the wick. Then he took Ginny's arm and ushered her through the door, locking it and pocketing the key.

The half-moon cast a silvery light over the town, and the preacher's heart seemed to swell within him when he looked at Ginny in the moonlight. He found her truly enchanting. "A lady shouldn't be walking the streets alone at night, Mrs. Wheeler," he told her. "If I may have your permission, I'll walk you home."

Ginny Wheeler looked into his eyes, as if to assess his intentions—although Harrigan was sure that she would be reluctant to let anything develop between them after all the hurt she had suffered. Then, apparently having made a decision to raise the barrier she had erected within herself, the young widow answered, "Yes, you may walk me home."

Reaching her house, they were standing on the porch and Harrigan's arms ached to hold her. He had to force himself to be content with shaking her hand when she offered it to him, saying, "Good night, Pastor. Thank you for walking me home."

Harrigan gave her hand a slight squeeze and then let go. "The pleasure has been mine," he said softly. "Good night."

She opened the door and slipped inside, and he started up the pathway. Pausing briefly, he looked back at the closed door, thinking about the struggle he sensed was going on inside her. He hoped it would soon be resolved—and he also hoped that she would, in time, see that he was not at all like Mack Wheeler. One thing was sure: If she belonged to him, she would never be hurt like that again.

Marshal Teal Peck and Del Harrigan breakfasted together at the Dakota Belle Café. When he'd heard about the incident in the town hall the evening before, Peck had gone looking for George Willoughby, Jud Beakins, and Alfie Downs before meeting the preacher, but they were nowhere to be found. Over breakfast the young marshal asked Harrigan how he wished to proceed, and Peck was extremely surprised when Harrigan told him he was not interested in pressing charges against the three troublemakers. Since no one had been hurt, Harrigan explained, he preferred to just let it go. He believed that if matters went no further, the three men would let sleeping dogs lie.

When the marshal had finished eating, he excused himself, saying he had work to do. He stepped outside and headed for his office across the street. As he did, he suddenly heard the sound of hooves pounding rapidly down the street and turned to see the town's hostler, young Jimmy Boyd, galloping toward him, frantically waving his hat.

"Marshal! Marshal!" shouted Boyd, his long yellow hair flying in the wind.

Peck stopped in the middle of the street as the hostler pulled his horse to a halt. "What's wrong, Jimmy?" he asked.

Gasping for breath, his pale blue eyes bulging with fear, Boyd said, "They're comin'!"

"Who's coming?"

"The Sioux!" exclaimed Boyd, pointing eastward. "It's Eagle Claw, and he's got a passel of warriors with him!

They're headed this way! We gotta warn the people before they get here!"

Peck's face went white. "How close are they?"

"Maybe five miles. They're ridin' slow, though, and don't seem to be in a hurry."

Panic surged through the young marshal's body. Speaking past the tightness in his throat, he declared, "They've probably come to get that old Sioux at Doc Curtin's office. Eagle Claw's a mean one. He may want to shed some blood while he's doing it. We've got to work fast!"

The marshal and the hostler dashed up and down the street, warning the townspeople of the coming danger. The Sioux warriors had returned from Montana and were on their way to Red Buffalo.

Del Harrigan jumped up from his table. Along with the other people in the café, he hurried out to see what was going on, discovering that men were arming themselves and pushing wagons together to form a barricade across the street.

Harrigan caught the marshal as he rushed about shouting orders and asked, "Do I understand right? A band of Sioux warriors is headed this way?"

"Yes!" Peck confirmed, nodding. "And Eagle Claw—one of their fiercest chiefs—is leading them!"

"Maybe he just wants to check on Lone Fox," suggested Harrigan calmly.

"That's possible, I guess," replied the marshal, although his expression said otherwise. "But he may come looking for blood."

Throwing a glance at the barricade, Harrigan said, "Since I'm the one who brought Lone Fox to Doc Curtin for treatment, maybe I ought to ride out and meet Eagle Claw. I'm sure the children gave him the whole story, so Eagle Claw will know I'm a friend to Lone Fox."

"That might not make any difference," argued the marshal. "It was white men who beat up on the old man to begin with, so Eagle Claw might just decide to kill you first."

"That's a chance I guess I'll have to take," Harrigan

decided, heading for a horse that was tied in front of the café. "If he's thinking of bloodshed, maybe I can change his mind."

Several of the townsmen had heard the conversation between the marshal and the preacher. As they watched Del Harrigan mount the borrowed horse and head eastward up the street, the men took their places behind the barricade and waited to see what would happen. Word of the preacher's effort soon spread throughout the town, even reaching the men, women, and children who were huddled in their homes in dread of a Sioux attack.

Trotting out of town, Del Harrigan told himself that if Lone Fox knew English, then Eagle Claw no doubt did, too. Communication should be no problem; he just hoped the chief would give him the *chance* to talk.

He was little more than a mile out of town when he saw the band of Sioux heading toward him, and he slowed his horse to a walk. As he drew closer, Harrigan had no trouble picking out Eagle Claw. The formidable-looking chief, his muscular bronze body glistening in the sun, sat astride a spirited white horse. A long ceremonial headdress framed his solemn face. He wore a necklace of wolf fangs, and heavy bracelets circled his upper arms, but other than his beaded moccasins, he was clad only in a breechcloth.

Harrigan did a quick body count. The warriors followed their chief four abreast and there were nine rows of them. There was also a stern-looking Sioux in a smaller headdress riding at Eagle Claw's right hand, whom Harrigan figured to be a war chief. That made a total of thirty-eight Sioux in all.

As the preacher drew abreast of the Sioux band, he lifted his right hand in the universal sign of peace. Eagle Claw made the same gesture and reined in his horse.

"You are Chief Eagle Claw?" asked Harrigan.

The somber-faced Indian nodded. Then he spoke, his voice deep and matter-of-fact. "You are the white-eyes who fought against your brothers to protect Lone Fox."

99

Harrigan realized that Lone Fox's great-grandchildren must have given the chief a good description of him. He nodded. "Yes. My name is Del Harrigan. I am the minister of Red Buffalo's Community Church. Do you understand my words?"

Eagle Claw replied, "Mmm. You are a messenger of the Great Spirit in sky."

"That's it," Harrigan agreed, smiling. Then he asked, "Are you going to Red Buffalo to see about Lone Fox?"

Harrigan was relieved that the chief's face did not show anger. But although the warriors arrayed behind him remained stoical, the fearsome-looking warrior who sat next to Eagle Claw had a hostile look in his eyes.

Eagle Claw answered, "That is correct. We have come to take Lone Fox home."

Harrigan quickly described Lone Fox's serious condition, explaining that the elderly Sioux would indeed recover, but that it would be weeks before he could travel to the village. The preacher assured the chief that Lone Fox was safe in Dr. Curtin's clinic and that no harm would come to him.

The chief grunted, "I will go to see Lone Fox."

"That will be fine, Eagle Claw," Harrigan assured him, knowing that the chief would feel better about the situation if he could talk to the old man.

Eagle Claw turned to the man at his right and said, "Fighting Bear, you will stay here with these braves. I will go with this messenger of the Great Spirit and talk to Lone Fox."

Fighting Bear nodded wordlessly but gave Del Harrigan a suspicious look as he and the chief nudged their horses toward town.

When the two riders reached the end of Main Street, the men of Red Buffalo peered at them from behind the barricade. When Harrigan quickly explained to Eagle Claw that the townspeople had feared the Indians were coming to attack, the chief did not comment. The preacher then asked some of the men to remove part of the barricade, and a wagon was quickly rolled out of the way. As the two men rode slowly along Main Street, Harrigan could see that from behind dusty shop windows the citizens of Red Buffalo were keeping watchful eyes on the Sioux chieftain.

The tension had increased by the time they reached the clinic, but after going inside and seeing that Lone Fox was being well taken care of, Eagle Claw appeared to be more at ease. The old man assured his chief that he was being treated kindly, and, satisfied, Eagle Claw smiled and nodded. He told Lone Fox he would visit him again, and after thanking Del Harrigan for his help, the two men went outside and remounted their horses. They rode slowly back along Main Street, and the Sioux chief headed back to his warriors and his village, while Harrigan advised everyone at the barricade that all was well.

The good news spread as quickly as the warning had, and the people poured out of the shops and stores along the street. Gathering around Del Harrigan, they expressed their gratitude for what he had done to spare the town from a Sioux attack. When Ginny Wheeler came over to praise him for his courage, the preacher noticed Frank Meeker watching with envy. The stationmaster's expression changed from envy to anger when Harrigan invited Ginny to dine with him that evening and she warmly accepted.

Watching her go, Del Harrigan shrugged off the younger man's reaction. *Sorry, Frank,* he told himself. *Apparently you're smitten yourself with Ginny—and who would not be?—but the lady made it quite clear that she does not return your affections . . . which means I'm free to pursue them myself.*

Del Harrigan took Ginny Wheeler to what he had been told was the nicest restaurant in town—which, he decided with some amusement, would make most of the people he had left behind in Philadelphia raise their eyebrows at the very thought.

When they walked home in the moonlight, the preacher felt his heart pounding so hard against his ribs, he was sure Ginny could hear it. They stepped onto her front porch and sat beside each other on a wicker settee, and Harrigan once again had to force himself not to sweep her into his arms.

They talked for a while longer, and Harrigan was finding Ginny more and more irresistible. Furthermore, he was quite sure that she was feeling the same way about him. Realizing it had grown quite late, he stood up to leave and impulsively took her in his arms.

Suddenly the barrier that Ginny Wheeler had tried to erect melted, and she hugged him, holding him so tightly that it left him speechless. But then the old reserve slipped back into place, and she pulled away. Not wanting to frighten her any more, he gave her a light kiss on the cheek, saying, "Sleep well, Ginny. And pleasant dreams."

Watching him go, Ginny sighed and leaned against the door. Then she went inside and suddenly began to weep. "Why did I let myself do that? I'm a fool for letting things go so far." Stomping through the hallway to her bedroom, she declared, "I will not let it happen again, and I will not allow myself to be hurt any more." Flinging back the bedcovers, she jabbed a fist into her pillow, saying forcefully, "A few minutes of pleasure are not worth all the pain that follows."

Chapter Ten

It was just before noon when Reverend Del Harrigan finished his Sunday sermon and proceeded to collect the special pledges that had been made by the congregation during the midweek service. As the plates were being passed among the congregation, an elderly woman parishioner played a rousing hymn on the pump organ. Standing behind the pulpit, Harrigan watched his parishioners donating generously and smiled. They had rallied to him far more quickly than he had expected—knowing how much Cletus Burke had meant to them—and he was proud that they had accepted him so readily.

Just as the ushers were handing the offering plates to the pastor, the door crashed open, slamming hard against the wall. The pump organ ceased playing as George Willoughby, Jud Beakins, and Alfie Downs thundered in. Standing by the open doorway waving revolvers, the three men commanded that no one move, and the parishioners froze in their seats.

Del Harrigan ground his teeth with fury at this second intrusion and quickly placed the offering plates behind the lectern.

Beakins and Downs, each holding two guns, remained near the door. They kept the crowd covered while Willoughby swaggered up the aisle, his weapon trained on the preacher. When he reached the foot of the lectern, Willoughby bellowed, "I want the money, Reverend!"

Harrigan shrugged. "I don't know what you're talking about."

Holding his revolver steady, Willoughby grinned evilly and rasped, "The money you collected here today, Harrigan. We heard about the special offerin' these folks was gonna make to build a new church. Well, me and my friends are gonna build us a new life, instead." Thumbing back the hammer on the revolver, the man demanded, "Hand it over right now, Preacher, or you're a dead man!"

Harrigan's right hand was hidden from Willoughby's view behind the pulpit as it had been on Wednesday night. Standing erect, the preacher glared at the intruder and said coldly, "I can drop you before you can blink. Put the gun down and reach for the ceiling."

Willoughby's shoulders shook as he chuckled. Sneering, he told the minister, "I heard it bandied around town how you was bluffin' last time. Well, you must think I'm real stupid if you think I'd fall for that stupid bluff a second time." With fire in his eyes, he roared, "I want the money, Harrigan! Right now!"

"I'm giving you one more chance, mister," warned Harrigan. "Drop the gun or take a bullet!"

Jud Beakins shouted from the rear of the room, "Hurry up, George! Kill him and take the money! Let's get outta here!"

Willoughby's mouth tightened into a thin line, and he defiantly raised his revolver, aiming the muzzle between Harrigan's eyes.

A gun roared, and the parishioners screamed, jumping in fright—but it was George Willoughby who howled, falling to the floor in pain. The .44 caliber slug from Del Harrigan's weapon left a splintered path through the pulpit where it had ripped through the wood on its way to Willoughby's thigh.

Before Willoughby's two stunned cohorts could react, Harrigan's revolver was in plain view, pointed in their direction. Acrid blue smoke rose from the pulpit as the angry preacher blared, "Drop your guns, you two, or you're next!"

Staring in disbelief at the smoking weapon, Beakins and Downs eased down the hammers of their guns and let the weapons fall to the floor.

Several of the parishioners hurriedly gathered the men's revolvers, and Marshal Peck was summoned. With the help of a couple of men, the marshal hauled the would-be thieves off to jail, assuring Harrigan before he left the town hall, "Don't worry, Reverend, they won't be bothering you again. As soon as the circuit judge comes through town, they'll be standing trial for robbery and attempted murder."

Three days later, ground was broken and a foundation was laid for the new church building. The men in the church donated as much of their time as they could to the construction, and—much to Del Harrigan's surprise and pleasure—even Red Buffalo townsmen who were not members of the church pitched in. By the following Sunday, the entire framework was up, ready for the roof and walls.

Early Monday morning, Reverend Harrigan and two other men climbed to the top of the wooden framework and began nailing on the roof. It was midmorning when, from his high perch, Harrigan watched four riders as they came into town. They rode steadily closer, and when they were almost directly below the building he suddenly stopped hammering.

One of the other workers was coming up a ladder with a bundle of shingles on his shoulder. The other one was on the ground, filling his apron pockets with roofing nails. When Harrigan's pounding abruptly stopped, both men paused and looked up at him. When they saw him staring down at the road, they followed his line of sight and looked at the four riders.

"Buffalo hunters!" exclaimed the man on the ladder.

Del Harrigan had never in his life laid eyes on a buffalo hunter, but he had guessed what these four men were before he heard it confirmed. All of them were dressed in dirty buckskins, and they looked like they hadn't shaved or bathed in months. In all his days, he had

105

never seen such scruffy, unsavory-looking men—he thought they could almost be a breed apart—and he now understood why the citizens of Red Buffalo were so fearful of these people.

The man on the ground watched them ride by and then looked up at Harrigan and said, "There'll be trouble in town now. You can bet your bottom dollar on it."

"I'm not a betting man," the preacher said lightly, looking down at him with a smile.

"There's still gonna be trouble," replied the man, trying to smile back as he said it.

Harrigan started driving nails again, focusing on the task at hand, but his mind was on Teal Peck. He wondered if the youthful lawman could handle four men as tough as those buffalo hunters looked to be.

Less than a quarter hour had passed when the three-man construction crew saw a teenage boy running toward them. His eyes held a worried look, and there was fear stamped on his face.

The three men again paused in their labors, and one of the men explained to Harrigan, "That's Henry Duggan's boy, Mark. I wonder what's wrong."

Mark ran up, shouting, "Reverend Harrigan, Reverend Harrigan! My pa told me to come and get you!"

"What's the matter?" Harrigan called down to him—although he had a sinking feeling that he already knew what it was.

"Some buffalo hunters just rode into town, and they're causing real trouble!" cried the youth. "Hurry, please!"

Del Harrigan had never refused to help anyone in trouble, but he was a bit perturbed that he was being called upon to handle a problem that belonged to the man who wore the badge. "What about Marshal Peck? Isn't he in town?" the preacher asked.

"Yes," gasped the Duggan boy, "but the buffalo hunters took his gun away from him, and they've got him tied to the rear of my pa's delivery wagon!"

Harrigan shook his head in disgust and started down

the ladder. The youth added, "They've also grabbed two women, and they're huggin' and kissin' them!"

"What two women?" asked the preacher, feeling his anger rising.

"Mrs. Taylor and my teacher!"

Harrigan's feet touched the ground and his body stiffened. "Your teacher? You mean Mrs. Wheeler?"

"Yes, sir."

Harrigan took off on a dead run, leaving the two crewmen and the boy lagging way behind.

Racing onto the scene, Harrigan saw that Teal Peck was indeed tied to the rear of the delivery wagon, and standing in front of him, taunting him, were two of the buffalo hunters; the other two were passing Ginny Wheeler and Shirley Taylor between them. The two women were weeping and struggling against the strong, filthy hands of the men who embraced and forced kisses on them. Two townsmen who had apparently tried to interfere were lying facedown in the dusty street, moaning; one of them was Henry Duggan. The rest of the crowd that had gathered stood meekly watching, and it was clear they were afraid to rile the burly hunters.

The tears on Ginny's face and the terror in her eyes created a storm of wrath inside the preacher. Without a word, he flew at the hunter who held her and jabbed a thumb into his right eye. The big man howled in agony. When he released Ginny to put both hands to his burning eye, she jumped to safety, and Harrigan unleashed a smashing blow to the hunter's midsection. When the man took his hands away from his face, he took another punch to the jaw and went down as though he had been hit with a sledgehammer.

Seeing his friend attacked, the man who had been holding Shirley Taylor let her go and moved in swinging. Harrigan saw him coming and tried to dodge him, but the hunter caught him on the shoulder with the first punch. The man missed with the second, and Harrigan chopped the hunter in the throat with the blade of his right hand. While the man gasped and gagged in pain, Harrigan

seized him by the collar and the seat of his pants and used
him as a battering ram, driving him headlong into the
other two hunters, who were charging at him. All three
went down in a heap, swearing, although only one stayed
down, still gagging. The other two stumbled to their feet
with fire in their eyes, and Harrigan heard Ginny pleading
with the bystanders to help him—but nobody moved.

As the two men stalked toward him, Harrigan looked
around for a weapon. He spied the hunters' nearby horses,
and each of their saddles had a boot bearing a single-shot
.50 caliber Sharps rifle. But even the closest horse was too
far away to get to in time. Then he noticed, sticking up
out of the Duggan wagon some six feet away, a length of
two-by-four.

Leaping over to the wagon just as the two men thundered in, he grabbed the piece of lumber. Swinging the
makeshift club, Harrigan caught the closest hunter square
in the mouth, splitting his lips and mashing his teeth. The
man went down, but the other one charged, screaming
profanities.

Off balance from swinging the two-by-four, Harrigan
was unable to keep the hunter from rushing in under the
club, and the man drove his head into his stomach. Both
men hit the ground and Harrigan lost his grip on the
two-by-four. They threshed about, rolling over and over in
the dust.

The hunter whose throat had been injured now got
up and came to help his friend. Finally breaking free from
the man he was wrestling, Harrigan seized the two-by-four
and flung it hard against the shins of the other two, who
were charging at him. While they stumbled about, Harrigan
got the chance to dash to the closest horse and yank the
buffalo rifle from its boot, praying it was loaded. Snapping
back the hammer, he swung the muzzle at the hunters
and bellowed, "Hold it right there!"

The two who were on their feet stopped and glared at
Harrigan. One of them snarled, "You ain't gonna use that
gun. I heard these folks say you're a preacher—and I ain't

never heard of no preacher who'd kill his fellow man."
While he spoke, he was drawing his revolver.

Knowing he had no choice, Harrigan dropped the
hammer. The Sharps boomed and the man flopped back-
wards from the impact of the .50 caliber slug, which went
clear through his body.

The other man clawed for his pistol. With all his
might, Harrigan hurled the Sharps at him. Then he dashed
to another one of the hunters' horses and pulled out
another buffalo gun. Clutching his chest where the rifle
had struck him, the hunter froze in his tracks when he saw
another gun cocked and trained on him. His expression
said that he knew the preacher would use the gun if he
had to.

Gasping for breath, Harrigan shouted to the goggle-
eyed crowd, "Somebody untie the marshal—and grab
their weapons." When the hunters had been disarmed and
their other rifles confiscated, Harrigan hissed at them,
"Pick up your dead pal and get out of town right now—
and don't ever come back!"

The men did as they were told, and Harrigan held
the buffalo gun on them until they disappeared from sight.
Then he dropped it to the ground.

With tears streaming down her cheeks, Ginny Wheeler
rushed to the tall man and embraced him, crying, "Oh,
Del, thank God you're all right! I don't how to thank you
for saving me from those horrible, filthy beasts!"

Del Harrigan was glad to be able to hold Ginny in his
arms, even if it was only for a moment. She pulled away
when Shirley Taylor and Teal Peck came up to him,
thanking him heartily for what he had done.

With Ginny standing beside him, Harrigan watched the
subdued young marshal walk slowly toward his office. It
was evident that Peck was low on experience—and possibly on courage.

Feeling Ginny trembling, the preacher looked into
her tearful eyes and told her tenderly, "You look a little
peaked. Let me see you home."

"All right," she agreed, brushing her disheveled hair

from her face. A shudder ran through her body. "I'm going to run a bath and scrub myself with strong soap." She ran a hand over her mouth, adding with disgust, "And rinse out my mouth with gargle. Those filthy animals *kissed* me." She shuddered again, and her face paled.

With his hand protectively touching her back, Del Harrigan escorted Ginny Wheeler to her home. Reaching the porch, Ginny turned and asked, "May I fix you a cup of coffee?"

"Sure," he rejoined, smiling. "But I'll have to drink it and run. Got to get back to my roofing job."

Harrigan sat at the kitchen table while Ginny put the coffeepot over a hastily made fire. "There," she sighed as she turned away from the stove. "It'll be ready in a minute." Walking toward him, she stood beside his chair looking at him with tear-filled eyes. "I was really frightened when you were fighting those awful men. I was afraid they were going to kill you. I . . . I . . ."

The tall man stood up, towering over her, his heart drumming against his ribs. "I liked holding you earlier," he whispered.

The beautiful brunette blushed, and their eyes locked for a long moment. Harrigan could read Ginny's longing to kiss him, and he moved close and took her in his arms. But he could also feel her ambivalence, and he could almost see the wall coming up between them as fear welled up in her mind.

Ginny stiffened, and Harrigan immediately let go of her, saying, "I'm sorry, Ginny. I didn't mean to—"

Reaching out and touching his arm, she said quickly, "No! Please don't think that I didn't want you to. I . . . mean— Oh, Del!" As she spoke, Ginny moved back into his arms and laid her head on his massive chest. "Del . . . I'm so mixed up, so very confused. Something is happening between us, and I'm afraid of it."

Pressing her closely to him, the tall man laid a gentle hand on the back of her head and said, "Ginny, I understand."

Fighting tears, she asked, "You do?"

110

"Yes. You're afraid to . . . to let it happen because it might mean getting hurt like before. With Mack, I mean. Right?"

Sniffling slightly, she nodded wordlessly.

He embraced her for a long moment, savoring the sweetness of holding her in his arms. He wanted desperately to tell her that he was in love with her, but he knew it was not the time to do so. Not wanting to make her uncomfortable again, he told her lightly, "I'd guess the coffee is just about ready," and released her.

"Oh, yes," she breathed, and moved to the stove.

Harrigan drank his coffee and then asked if he could take her to dinner that evening. She accepted and walked him to the door. Looking down at her tenderly, he said, "Ginny, I want to say one thing; then I'll go."

Looking steadily into his eyes, she asked, "And what is that, Del?"

"If you belonged to me, I would never hurt you. Never."

After Harrigan and Ginny had dined together at the hotel restaurant, he walked her home as a three-quarter moon cast its silvery light over the prairie town. When they reached the house and stood at the edge of the porch, he looked into her eyes and, tenderly brushing away a stray lock of hair from her face, told her, "Thank you for letting me take you to dinner. I'll see you tomorrow."

The fear of being hurt again still clawed at Ginny Wheeler's mind, but she also knew that her bruised and battered heart was finding solace with this gentle, kind man. His last words earlier in the day had echoed through her mind all afternoon: *If you belonged to me, I would never hurt you. Never. . . .*

It came like an abrupt cloudburst. Suddenly Ginny knew she was in love with Del Harrigan—deeply and desperately in love. And she knew without any doubt that he, indeed, would never hurt her.

As he started to turn away, Ginny reached out and laid a hand on his arm. "Do you have to go so quickly?"

She wanted him to hold her, to kiss her, to put into word the feelings she had read in his expressive eyes.

Harrigan paused. "I can stay if you want me to," h replied with a smile.

"I want you to," she breathed.

He reached out and pulled her to him, folding he into his strong arms. As he lowered his head she close her eyes and lifted her lips to his. At the touch of his lips her heart seemed to burst into flame, and they kissed lon and lovingly. When their lips parted, they looked int each other's eyes, then kissed again, a kiss so warm an sweet that the young schoolteacher felt she would savor it memory forever. Her hand went up to the back of hi head, and she sank her fingers into his thick hair an pulled his mouth firmly against hers.

When the kiss ended, Harrigan held her close an whispered into her ear, "Ginny, I'll explode if I don't sa what I'm feeling. I'm in love with you. I've known almost since the first time I saw you."

Her breath caught in her throat, and she felt tear coursing down her cheeks. Snuggling against his chest she whispered back, "I'm in love with you, too, my dar ling. I've never met a man like you. Oh, I love you, Del. love you so very much."

They kissed tenderly again, the handsome man cup ping her face in his hands. Wiping away her tears, he tol her, "Ginny, I pledge to you here and now that you wil always have my heart. You will have my love and devotio until the day I die."

Ginny held him tightly and wept for joy. "Oh, Del, she sniffed, "I'm so happy! So incredibly happy! I neve knew I could feel like this!"

He drew back slightly and looked into her eyes. Smil ing, he suggested, "Well, we might as well get this settle completely here and now. Ginny Wheeler, I want you t be my wife. Will you marry me?"

Her face was shiny with tears as she looked up a him, unable to speak. Reaching into his hip pocket, Harriga withdrew a handkerchief and handed it to her. She dabbe at her tears, and her lower lip quivered as she replied shakily, "I would feel so honored to marry you, but I . . . I . . ."

"What is it, my sweet?" he asked gently.

She looked down, unable to meet his gaze. "I . . . well, a minister's wife has to be someone special, and I'm afraid I . . . I'm just not good enough to fill those shoes."

"Not good enough!" he exclaimed. "Ginny, darling, you're more than good enough! Why, there isn't a soul in this town who doesn't adore you. Oh, my dear, you're perfect for what I need in a wife. In every way. I mean that! Please say you will marry me."

She looked up at him and smiled, shyly at first, then beaming. "You're as persuasive out of the pulpit as you are in it, Reverend Harrigan. If you will have me as I am, then yes, darling, I will marry you."

Del Harrigan let out a whoop and scooped the laughing Ginny Wheeler into his arms, both of them elated beyond words. He kissed her several times. Then he said, "Let's talk about a wedding date soon, all right?"

Ginny was about to answer when the sound of a galloping horse interrupted her. Harrigan set her down on the porch just as the rider pulled to a stop in front of the house and slid from the saddle. In the moonlight they saw it was Jimmy Boyd, the hostler.

"Reverend Harrigan!" the youth shouted excitedly. "We got trouble!"

Turning to meet him, Harrigan asked, "What is it, Jimmy?"

"George Willoughby, Jud Beakins, and Alfie Downs have broken out of the jail! Somehow they tricked Marshal Peck and overpowered him. They locked him up in a cell and then stole three horses from my stable. I saw them ridin' off just as I happened to look out my window. That's when I ran down to the jail and found Marshal Peck locked up."

Shaking his head, Harrigan commented, "I don't understand, Jimmy. Why have you come to me? Isn't Peck going to form a posse and go after them?"

"I'm comin' to you, Reverend," replied Boyd, "because Marshal Peck has resigned. As soon as I let him out of the cell, he went to his desk and wrote a letter of resignation. He told me to give it to the town council, and then he threw his badge on the desk and rode out of town. He's gone."

Harrigan rubbed a hand across his face and said, "Jimmy, I'm sorry, but you've come to the wrong man. I'm a preacher, not a lawman."

"But there's more," gasped Boyd. "I just found out those three scoundrels then swung around to Doc Curtin's clinic. They broke in and kidnapped that old Indian!"

Harrigan's mouth fell open. "They've got Lone Fox?"

"Yes, sir."

Ginny saw the indecision on Harrigan's face as he ran his fingers through his hair. "Del, what are you going to do?" she asked fearfully.

"Well," he answered, shaking his head, "there's obviously going to be real trouble now." He paused and pulled out his pocket watch. "It's almost midnight . . . but I'm going to see if I can't round up some men and form a posse." He looked at the youth. "Jimmy, you can help me. We'll talk to them tonight so we can be ready to leave at dawn." His gaze drifted out over the prairie, and he added, "We've got to ride those three devils down before they do anything to Lone Fox."

Chapter Eleven

The first glow of morning was washing over the Dakota plains when Henry Duggan, as chairman of the town council, swore in ten men as a posse and deputized Del Harrigan to lead them. "Let's move out, men!" Harrigan shouted, and the eleven men started toward the doctor's office. Halting the posse far enough away from the clinic so as not to disturb whatever tracks were visible, the preacher quickly determined that the outlaws and their prisoner had headed south out of Red Buffalo.

"All right, men, follow me," Harrigan ordered, clucking to his horse.

As the procession neared the southern edge of town, the schoolhouse came into view, and next to it, the framework of the new church building. A dark form high among the rafters suddenly caught Harrigan's eye and, reining in his horse, he squinted at it. He gasped, and the hair on the back of his neck bristled as his eyes focused on the body of a man, hanging by his neck from a rope. It was Lone Fox. Following the direction of his gaze, the other men saw what he was looking at, and a murmur of disbelief rose up from the posse.

The preacher's rugged face registered his shock, and the quivering that started in the pit of his stomach raced throughout his body. Spurring their horses, Harrigan and the men galloped to the front of the church building and dismounted. Looking up at Lone Fox's corpse, its blackened tongue protruding obscenely, the preacher could see that the old man's arms had been cruelly wrenched behind his back and tied.

Some of the men swore and then apologized to the preacher for their language, explaining that this was surely going to bring the wrath of Eagle Claw down on the town.

Harrigan had hardly heard the profanity. He was feeling sick all over as he thought of how he had assured the Sioux chieftain that Lone Fox was safe at Doc Curtin's clinic. He regretted not having insisted that guards be posted at the clinic.

"What are we gonna do, Reverend?" asked one of the men, his voice catching.

Harrigan stroked his mustache. With his eyes still fixed on the hanging Indian, he observed, "As I see it, the only possible way to prevent bloodshed over this is to send a citizen of Red Buffalo right to Eagle Claw to tell him about it. If the chief should ride in and find out from some other source, there's no question he'll come at us ready for war."

The preacher directed three of the men to cut Lone Fox down and then told everyone, "I think it's best that I be the one to bear the news to Eagle Claw, since he knows me, and perhaps I've gained his confidence somewhat."

One of the men said, "That's going to be risky business, Reverend. Even bearing the news could prove dangerous—if not fatal. Eagle Claw might just decide to chop you up into little pieces right on the spot."

Harrigan shrugged his shoulders. "Believe me, gentlemen, I'm not at all thrilled about walking into the Sioux stronghold—but unless you can come up with a better idea, I have no choice."

No one spoke.

Shrugging again, the tall man said, "Well, I guess that settles it. I'll take the bad news to Eagle Claw. If the Lord is willing and my explanation rings true to the chief, maybe he won't make war on Red Buffalo."

After the corpse had been cut down and wrapped in a large piece of canvas that had covered some building materials, Harrigan told the men to hide it at the rear of the building amid the stacks of lumber. The murder had to remain a secret until Harrigan could get to Eagle Claw with the news. Then, as soon as he could, he would return the body to the Sioux village for a proper burial.

The preacher was then struck with another problem. Willoughby, Beakins, and Downs had to be caught as soon as possible and brought back to face trial for murder— but no one in the posse could be counted on to lead the men. And without strong and capable leadership, they would never track down and bring in the culprits.

Reasoning his mission might be easier if he could tell the chief that Lone Fox's killers were in custody and were going to be punished to the fullest extent of the law, Harrigan decided to continue with the pursuit first. The preacher explained his plan to the men, and they mounted up and rode out of town at a gallop.

When George Willoughby's thigh wound had torn open from riding and begun to bleed profusely, the three fugitives had been forced to hole up in an abandoned barn some twenty miles south of Red Buffalo. The dilapidated structure was at the bottom of a draw some fifty yards from the road, not visible to anyone traveling on the road, but Alfie Downs had spotted it while hunting for something to eat the night before.

Lying on the dirt floor of the barn, Willoughby gritted his teeth and swore as Jud Beakins attempted to tighten the bloodied bandage.

"Sorry, George," Jud said. "I know it hurts like hell, but we've got to get the bleeding stopped before you plumb run out of blood."

"I'm not swearin' at you, old pal," breathed Willoughby. "I'm just swearin' at the goddamn pain." Relaxing somewhat, a wicked grin spread over his mouth and he added, "But it's almost worth all this pain just to know we sent that stinkin' old Sioux to his happy huntin' ground."

Alfie Downs chuckled. "I wonder if the holy reverend's found him yet. That sure was a good idea, George, hangin' him from the reverend's new church roof. Wish we coulda been there to see his face."

Looking serious, Beakins cut in, "George, I sure hope your bleedin' stops pretty soon, 'cause we need to stay on the move. It won't take them people in Red Buffalo long to find their stupid marshal. Peck'll get up a posse and come after us, you know that."

"Guess we should've killed him, too," put in Downs

"Don't make no difference," declared Willoughby "Peck's as slow as molasses in January, anyhow. It'll take him a good while to form a posse. And scared as he is, it'll take him even longer to get up the guts to light onto our trail. I'll give it till dawn tomorrow. Bleedin' should be stopped by then. If not, you boys'll just have to go on and leave me here."

"Not on your life, George," Jud Beakins said firmly "We ain't leavin' you. Right, Alfie?"

"Right," responded the little man. "Anyhow, that won't be necessary. The bleedin' will stop by mornin', and we'll be able to pull out together at dawn."

The sun was lowering in the brassy sky when the Butterfield Overland Mail stagecoach pulled into Red Buffalo and rolled to a halt in front of the office. Frank Meeker came through the office door with a smile, greeting the driver and shotgunner, when his eyes were immediately drawn to the attractive young woman being helped from the coach by an older man. The late afternoon sun seemed to dance in her fiery red hair, and when she noticed him watching her, she nodded her head as accepting his appraisal. Meeker thought she wore rather too much makeup, but he told himself she was a real beauty beneath it all. He was sure she was a saloon woman.

Hand on hip, she approached Meeker and said with a smile, "I heard the driver say you're the Butterfield agent here, which means you probably know most everyone in town, don't you, sugar?"

"I know them all, ma'am," boasted Meeker.

"Good," she replied, fluffing her hair. "Then you can tell me where to find a tall, handsome man by the name of Del Harrigan."

Meeker wondered why a woman of her station would have any connection with the preacher. But, always congenial with Butterfield passengers, he responded amiably, "He's out of town at the moment, ma'am. Is there something I can do for you?"

The smile left her lips as she asked, "When will he be back?"

"Hard to say, ma'am. He's riding with a posse after three men who broke jail last night. I'm sure he'll be back in a day or two."

Gazing up and down the street, she asked, "This town have any decent hotels?"

"We only have one hotel, ma'am," Meeker replied, "but it's a nice one." Pointing up the street, he told her, "That's it right over there—the building with the large porch. It's called The Red Buffalo Hotel."

"How original," she told him wryly. "Will you see to it that my luggage gets sent there?"

"Yes ma'am," Meeker assured her, smiling. "I didn't catch your name, ma'am. Who should I have the luggage delivered to?"

"Helen Coffman. Miss Helen Coffman."

Bernie Walker, the young hotel clerk, was on duty when the vivacious Helen Coffman floated into the lobby. He was instantly enamored of her flaming red hair and provocative figure. Walker's boyish face blushed when the woman stepped up to the desk and smiled at him.

"I'll need a room for a day or two, sugar. That won't be any problem, will it?"

"Oh, no, ma'am," Walker assured her, spinning the register around so she could sign it. As she picked up the pen and dipped it in the inkwell, he asked, "You're not sure whether it will be one day or two?"

"I'll only need the room until Del Harrigan returns with the posse. Do you know Del? He and I are very close friends."

"Yes, ma'am," Walker nodded. "I know him. As a matter of fact, for the time being he's living right here in the hotel."

Helen's thinly plucked eyebrows arched in surprise. "He is?"

"Yes, ma'am. Room twelve."

The redhead looked thoughtful for a moment. "Tell you what," she said, leaning close to Bernie Walker over the desk. "Like I told you, Del and I are very close friends. He won't mind at all if I stay in his room until he returns. After that, other arrangements can be made. May I have a key?"

Walker swallowed hard and scratched his head. "Well, ma'am," he began falteringly, "I don't know if I should do—"

"Oh, come on, honey," she breathed softly, batting her eyes suggestively. "It'll be all right, believe me."

The young clerk had difficulty imagining this woman in a close relationship with Reverend Harrigan, but he succumbed to her charm and waggled his head, saying, "Well, I guess it'll be okay if you say so, Miss Coffman."

Smiling, she told him, "Atta boy," and held out her hand for the key.

Walker placed it in her hand reluctantly and then directed, "It's the second room on the left-hand side, ma'am. Number twelve, as I said."

Helen thanked him and mounted the stairs, and soon Walker heard the key rattle in the door. The door squeaked open and then closed.

Some fifteen minutes later Frank Meeker came through the lobby door carrying two heavy suitcases and a small bag. Puffing and setting them down in front of the desk, he explained, "Bernie, these belong to Miss Coffman, a passenger on the stage, who should have checked in a while ago. What room is she in?"

Throwing a hasty glance toward the stairs, Walker leaned over the desk and replied in a low, confidential voice, "She's in room twelve . . . Reverend Harrigan's room. She insisted that she and Harrigan are *very* close friends, and that it would be all right if she stayed in his room until he returns."

Meeker's eyes bulged and his mouth fell open. Then, grinning wickedly, he finally exclaimed, "Well, I'll be! She asked me about Harrigan, but she didn't say anything about them being close friends." Lifting his eyes toward the second floor, he chuckled, "She's in his room, eh? Hmm. That's very interesting."

Saying no more, Frank Meeker carried the luggage up to room twelve and gave it to Helen Coffman. Tipping his hat to her politely, he then dashed down the stairs and out of the hotel, making a beeline for Ginny Wheeler's house. *Maybe when Ginny finds out that her loving preacher has a painted-up woman staying in his hotel room*, Meeker told himself, *I'll have a chance with her yet.*

Working in her flower garden, enjoying the sunset, the young schoolteacher looked up when the stationmaster appeared at the end of the pathway. From the way he was breathing, she was sure that he had been running.

"Good evening, Ginny," Meeker said as he walked up to the flower bed and stood beside the spot where she knelt. "I'm afraid I've got some bad news for you."

Ginny's heart leaped to her throat, and she immediately stood up. "Is it Del . . . I mean, Pastor Harrigan? Did something happen with the posse?"

"No, nothing like that," Meeker said evenly. "The posse is still out, and as far as I know, there hasn't been any word from them." Pausing a few seconds, he proceeded, "I hate to have to bring you this kind of news, but you certainly need to know it. That is, since you seem to have taken such a shine to our new . . . uh . . . *man of God.*"

Ginny stared at Meeker, her face hardening and her

mood along with it. "I don't like the tone of your voice, Frank."

"You haven't heard what I came to tell you yet, Ginny."

"Well, out with it," she demanded.

"Okay. When the stage came in a little while ago, there was a young woman on it, a woman named Helen Coffman. She's a real good-looker, but she wears a lot of rouge and powder and stuff. Kind of flirty, too, if you know what I mean. I'd guess she's a . . . lady of the night, if you get my point." Meeker stopped, obviously wanting to let the words sink in.

"What about her?" Ginny queried impatiently.

"She asked me if I could tell her where to find—and I'm quoting her, 'a tall, handsome man named Del Harrigan.' I explained that he was out with a posse and that he'd be back in a day or two."

Suddenly Frank Meeker had Ginny's full attention. "Did she say what she wanted with him?"

"No. She just asked about a hotel. I pointed out the Red Buffalo and she headed for it. *But* . . . when I took her luggage to the hotel a few minutes later, Bernie told me that she had insisted on staying in Harrigan's room, saying that they were very good friends and he wouldn't mind. She's there right now, in room number twelve."

Ginny felt her stomach tighten. Struggling as hard as she could to keep a casual expression on her face, she offered, "Maybe this Miss Coffman is just someone he's helped in the past. She might be exaggerating their so-called friendship somewhat. Those . . . painted women will do a thing like that, you know."

Meeker shrugged. "Well, think what you want, Ginny. I know you're sweet on him—but maybe he's not what he claims to be. You might be in for a big letdown . . . and I sure don't want to see you hurt again." The stationmaster moved close to the petite brunette and took hold of her shoulders, adding, "If you would let yourself fall in love with me, I would never hurt you, Ginny, never. I would always—"

"Don't, Frank!" she snapped, jerking free from his grasp. "I'm not going to listen to this talk about Del! There is a simple explanation for all this, and he will handle it when he comes back."

"*Del*, huh? That's twice you've called him by his Christian name. Maybe you're more than sweet on him."

Ginny's mind was spinning, and she was weary with Meeker's presence.

He pressed the point further. "Are you going to tell me that you're in love with your pastor, Ginny? Hmm? I mean, are you and the man of God—"

"You've given me your bad news, Frank!" she blurted roughly, cutting him off. "Now leave me alone!"

Meeker shook his head in exasperation. "Well, of all the ungrateful—"

He never got the chance to finish, for Ginny turned and dashed into the house, slamming the door.

Leaning against the door frame, Ginny Wheeler breathed deeply, trying to calm herself. It did not work, and she started pacing the floor, wringing her hands. There seemed to be a ball of fire in her stomach, and it was making her perspire heavily. Biting her lip, she realized she was getting the same awful feeling she had known so many times when Mack had been seeing other women. The knot in her throat tightened and, unable to hold back the sadness, she put her face in her hands and wept.

The sun had all but disappeared on the western horizon when a band of roughly thirty Sioux warriors, with the stony-faced Fighting Bear in the lead, rode slowly into Red Buffalo. They drew up in front of Dr. Jesse Curtin's office, and it was obvious to all the nervous bystanders that Eagle Claw had sent his war chief to town to check on Lone Fox.

Watching from his window, Dr. Curtin waited until the Sioux leader had dismounted. Then he stepped out of the office and walked down the pathway to meet him.

The Indian regarded the physician with cold black eyes. "I am here to talk to Lone Fox," he grunted.

Feeling ill with fear, Curtin cleared his throat and quickly told him that Lone Fox had been kidnapped by the same three men who had beaten him up after they had broken out of jail. Without waiting for a response, Curtin added that a posse had ridden out in pursuit of them.

Fighting Bear stared unwaveringly at the physician for a long moment, his fury almost palpable. Then he turned on his heel and strode back to his horse, leaping onto the animal's back and leading his men at a gallop back in the direction from which they had come.

Del Harrigan and his posse had followed the road heading south for the rest of the day, but the many wagons and horses using the road had long since obliterated any sign of the three killers. Harrigan could only guess that they were still headed in that direction, but with no further leads to follow, he felt he and his men had reached a dead end.

When darkness began to descend over the Dakota prairie, Harrigan drew rein. Turning to the ten men following suit, he told them, "I think they've given us the slip, gentlemen." Shaking his head, he continued, "I had figured for sure that with Willoughby's wound, they'd have had to travel relatively slow, and if they had stayed on the road, we'd have caught up to them by now."

"I think you're right," spoke up Cal Stearns, the town barber. "We've come about twenty-five miles already. I've got a feeling they left the road somewhere back there, and we missed the spot where they turned off."

"What are we gonna do?" asked Harry Ronders, a deacon of the church and the owner of Ronders' Saddle Shop.

Harrigan sighed, "We don't have much choice, Harry. I suggest that we camp over there by that creek tonight and then head back to town in the morning. It galls me to let those mangy dogs get away, but it's useless to push on any farther."

The others all agreed, and in the waning light, they pulled off the road and began to set up camp beside a narrow stream. Some of the men worked at getting a fire started, and still others broke out the cooking utensils and laid out the bedrolls. As Harrigan helped to unsaddle the horses, his attention was suddenly drawn toward the east. Jagged white bolts lit up the black sky.

"Heat lightning," commented Jake Green, Red Buffalo's gunsmith, who was working alongside Harrigan.

"It's beautiful, isn't it?" Harrigan mused. "It reminds me of the fireworks I watched back in Sioux City not long ago during the centennial celebration."

Green chuckled. "Well, who knows? Maybe some day Red Buffalo'll have its own fireworks to light up the sky."

By the time they had finished eating, the moon began to rise, but it was covered by low-lying clouds on the eastern horizon. The cooking utensils were washed in the stream, and then the men sat around in a circle by the glow of the campfire and discussed what would happen when Eagle Claw learned that Lone Fox had been murdered—and that his killers were at large.

"Reverend," Cal Stearns began, peering across at Harrigan, "are you still determined to go to the Sioux camp? It seems to me it's going to be suicide for you to ride into Eagle Claw's village and tell him Lone Fox was hanged by three white men and that we let them get away."

"Somebody's got to do it," replied Harrigan firmly, "and it'll certainly go better than if we let him find it out on his own."

"Maybe it would go better still if we arm about two hundred men and have them ride with you," Stearns added.

"I don't think so," replied the preacher. "That would only mean a show of strength to Eagle Claw, and he might take it as an act of aggression. No, I think my going in alone is the only way to handle it."

No one said anything more, and the silence was broken only by the crackling of the fire and the keening of the rising wind. Finally, everyone drifted over to the bedrolls, lost in thought about what tomorrow would bring, and soon all thoughts were erased by exhausted sleep.

Chapter Twelve

Morning came with a howling wind and the smell of smoke in the air. The possemen rose from their bedrolls and looked to the south to see a grass fire raging in the distance.

"Looks like a bad one," commented Harry Ronders.

"I sure hate to see one anywhere," said one of the others, "but at least there's no danger of this one hittin' town. That northerly wind is drivin' the fire farther south, away from Red Buffalo."

Everyone instinctively looked in the direction of the town, relieved that it would be safe.

After a quick breakfast, they saddled and mounted their horses and headed for home. They had ridden about five miles when Harry Ronders, who was riding in the lead with the pastor, saw movement farther ahead, just to the right of the road. Harrigan saw it a split second later. Suddenly they realized they were watching the three fugitives riding up out of a steep draw onto the road. From the way the trio was riding, it appeared that Willoughby, Beakins, and Downs had not spotted them yet.

"Hey, preacher!" one of the other men exclaimed in a hoarse whisper. "Do you see what I see?"

The others in the posse caught sight of the killers at the same time.

"Let's get 'em!" shouted one.

Del Harrigan drew his revolver and kicked his horse violently in the flanks, sending it into a gallop. The ten possemen followed right behind him, whipping out their own guns.

Alfie Downs spotted the posse first. They were close enough so that Harrigan could hear the man curse and then yell, "George, look! We gotta get outta here! That goddamn preacher's found us!"

But it was too late for escape. The posse was bearing down on them, guns ready for action. It was apparent that the threesome briefly thought about running, but then realizing it was hopeless, they reined in their mounts and waited for the thundering riders to close in and take them.

"Get those hands in the air!" bellowed Harrigan, pulling up on his horse as the posse quickly surrounded the killers and took their weapons. The preacher directed his men to tie the killers' hands, and while they were being bound, he growled, "You mangy dogs are going back to Red Buffalo to stand trial for murder."

"It ain't murder when you kill a stinkin' Indian," blustered George Willoughby, who sat crookedly in his saddle because of his wounded leg. "It ain't no different than killin' a rattlesnake. Why, look at what his people did to Custer and his men!"

"What you did was nothing short of cold-blooded murder," Cal Stearns declared, "and I don't care how you try to excuse it! But on top of that, what you did just might bring the whole Sioux nation down on us, you stupid fool. Our only chance to avoid that is to hang you—and hope to God that'll satisfy Eagle Claw."

After an hour or so on the trail, the procession was picking its way through an area where ravines, both shallow and deep, cut sinuous lines across the land. There was little talk among the men as they headed home, but suddenly every man in the group straightened in his saddle and gasped when, out of the surrounding gullies, rose a mass of Sioux warriors on horseback. The Indians came at them from every side, whooping loudly, their rifles poised and ready to fire.

Reining in his horse, Harrigan warned his men, "Don't try to resist! There are too many of them!"

Harrigan recognized the leader of the war party, Fighting Bear, and knew that the fact of Lone Fox's murder must come to light here and now. He had no idea what the outcome would be. He felt his chest constricting, felt the tension knotting inside him.

Both possemen and prisoners watched with wary eyes as the Indians pressed them into a tight circle. Fighting Bear guided his horse directly in front of the preacher, and there was clear malice in the war chief's jet-black eyes—malice, Harrigan knew, that would shortly intensify into rage.

"Where is Lone Fox?" the leader asked Del Harrigan in a deep guttural voice.

The preacher could sense every man in the posse stiffen with fear. He looked around; a quick count told him they were outnumbered three to one.

Then, meeting Fighting Bear's hard gaze, the preacher asked, "You have been to Red Buffalo?"

"Yes. Your medicine man told me these three men you captured escaped from jail and took Lone Fox with them." He paused, then asked again, even more harshly, "Where is Lone Fox?"

Fear stabbed through Del Harrigan's heart. He swallowed hard and admitted gravely, "Lone Fox is dead. These three men hanged him. We are taking them in to be punished. They will hang, also."

Fighting Bear looked as though he had been slapped. His copper face darkened, and he glared at Harrigan with eyes so fiery the preacher felt as if he might burst into flame. A terrible silence fell over white men and red men alike. Then the Sioux warrior barked, "Sioux justice must be done! You will turn the killers over to us!"

Harrigan knew that the three men would be tortured without mercy and then put to death slowly and painfully if the Indians took them. While he knew that what they had done was morally repugnant, he believed that no one should have to suffer an agonizing death at the hands of the Sioux.

Harrigan fought to hold his voice steady as he spoke. "Fighting Bear, I understand your anger, and it is entirely justified. But I cannot let you take these men. You have my word that they will be punished to the fullest extent of the law—which means they will be hanged."

Fighting Bear's features seemed to sharpen with his rage. "No!" he blared. "They must be punished according to Sioux law! They murdered Sioux, therefore they must answer to Sioux!"

Harrigan started to protest, but Fighting Bear cut in harshly, "My warriors will kill all of you right now if you do not let us take the killers of Lone Fox!"

A heavy silence fell on the group, broken only by the sound of a pony snorting. Harrigan felt the menace of thirty dark muzzles pointing at them. Behind the muzzles were faces filled with hate, warriors waiting only for their leader's word to cut down the despised white men. The preacher's blood ran cold in his veins.

He looked over at the three killers who sat in numb fear, sweat beading their brows—and he sensed that they knew what he was going to do.

Licking his lips, Harrigan looked over at Harry Ronders, whose face expressed very clearly what he was thinking. Then he turned and swept the faces of the other possemen with a slow, deliberate glance. There was no way he would let these good men die in an attempt to save the killers from the Sioux. It would be a futile effort, anyway. There would not be a single man left to tell the story if he tried to fight off these Indians. He had no choice—but he would give the men an opportunity to speak for themselves.

"What about it, men?" he asked.

Jake Green blurted, "Let 'em have 'em! We ain't got a chance, even if we wanted to spare these killers. Personally, I don't even want to."

The others voiced their agreement immediately.

Alfie Downs began to whimper wordlessly, a tear trickling down his cheek.

Jud Beakins seemed to have lost control of his tongue as he stammered, "H-Harrigan! Y-you c-c-c-can't let 'em take us! It . . . it ain't h-human! Th-these savages will t-torture us!"

"Yeah!" gasped Willoughby, anger mixing with fear. "You can't let 'em take us, Harrigan! We got a right to stand trial! You can't!"

"You forfeited any rights you had when you strung up that old man," Harrigan told them coldly. "And I don't see that it's right for these men to have to die trying to protect you. The Sioux have us cold, and we all know it." Turning to the war chief, he said resignedly, "Take them, Fighting Bear. We will not resist you."

The three killers united in a chorus of fearful pleas, begging Harrigan to do something. Shouting above their wails, Fighting Bear told Harrigan, "White preacher man better pray to his God that Chief Eagle Claw decides not to destroy Red Buffalo to avenge Lone Fox. White preacher man told Chief Eagle Claw that Lone Fox was safe—but it was a lie."

Harrigan remained silent, knowing it would be useless to try to explain that the kidnapping and murder of Lone Fox were tragic events beyond his control.

Saying no more, Fighting Bear spoke in his language to his braves, telling them to take the reins of the killers' horses. The war party then rode away with their terrified prisoners still screaming for help.

Waiting until the Sioux had passed from sight, Harrigan signaled his men, and the posse continued on its way to Red Buffalo.

Ginny Wheeler rose wearily from her bed at dawn after a restless, sleepless night. Having learned the evening before that Fighting Bear and his war party were out searching for Lone Bear's kidnappers, she was worried about the posse meeting up with the wrathful Sioux. But more than Fighting Bear's wrath had kept Ginny awake through the long hours of the night; she was extremely upset over the strange woman who had come to town asking for Del Harrigan and then been so brazen as to stay in his hotel room.

She bathed quickly and dressed. Walking distractedly to the bedroom window, she stood brushing her hair while watching the eastern sky grow lighter. She kept telling herself that this Helen Coffman mystery would be cleared up when Harrigan returned, that her faith in him was well founded . . . and that that brazen female would be sent packing. But as hard as she tried to convince herself that everything between the preacher and herself was going to be all right, she could not shake a vague feeling of dread, one she had experienced before when Mack was carrying on with other women.

Knowing she would have to keep her mind occupied until Harrigan returned, Ginny decided to go to the school-house and work on preparations for the opening of school which was only five weeks away. With a deep sigh, she made her way to the kitchen and ate a light breakfast, meticulously washing the dishes before she left. That done, she picked up her case full of papers and hurried across town to the schoolhouse. The building was very stuffy, and she opened the doors and all the windows. Then she sat at her desk and began the necessary paperwork.

After laboring for more than two hours, Ginny found that she was so distracted, thinking about Helen Coffman, that she was making mistakes and creating more work for herself than necessary. Finally, she decided to take the bull by the horns: She would go have a talk with the woman. Stacking her papers, she put them in the top drawer of her desk. Then she closed all the windows and locked the doors and headed for the hotel.

She entered the hotel lobby ten minutes later, and Bernie Walker looked up from his desk and greeted her. Although she tried to keep her face composed, she suspected that he knew she was upset.

Giving him a friendly smile, she said, "Good morning, Bernie."

"Good morning, Mrs. Wheeler," he responded, smiling in return. "How may I help you today?"

Ginny shot a glance up the stairs and then asked the clerk, "Is . . . is that woman still in Pastor Harrigan's room?"

"Why, uh, yes, she is. She was out for a little while earlier—I believe to get some breakfast—but then she went right back upstairs."

Ginny frowned. "I see. Tell me, which room is it, Bernie?"

"Number twelve."

Ginny was already walking toward the stairs as she said over her shoulder, "Thank you, Bernie." Lifting her skirts, she ascended the staircase and walked along the hallway until she reached the door of room number twelve. Taking a deep breath, she lifted her hand and, after a slight hesitation, rapped on the door. She could hear light footsteps inside, and then the knob rattled and the door opened. Ginny found herself momentarily aghast as she stared at what seemed to be an oversized, animated doll—or the redhead had on so much makeup that she did not look real, and her cloying perfume was so heavily applied that it fairly took the young schoolteacher's breath away.

Looking the brunette up and down impassively, Helen asked, "Is there something I can do for you?"

"Yes," replied Ginny without a hint of emotion. "We need to talk."

Helen leaned against the door frame, making it clear that whatever talking was to be done would take place right where they stood. "About what?"

"About Del Harrigan—and why you are staying in his room."

Helen's face hardened. Looking Ginny up and down again, she asked insolently, "What's it to you?"

"My name is Ginny Wheeler, and Del and I are engaged to be married. That's what."

If Ginny's words had any negative effect, the redhead did not reveal it. Instead she sneered and retorted, "Well, my name is Helen Coffman, and there's something fishy

133

going on here. Del and I have been lovers for . . . well none of your business how long, and I came here to marry him."

Helen Coffman's words pierced Ginny to the heart. Her eyes filled with tears, and she could think of nothing more to say. The old, painful wounds had been ripped open again. Biting her lip, she wheeled and hurried down the hallway and down the stairs. As she rushed through the lobby, wiping her tears, she was only barely aware of Bernie Walker looking at her askance.

Practically running all the way home, Ginny Wheeler dashed into the house, raced to the bedroom, and threw herself on the bed. She buried her face in a pillow and sobbed uncontrollably. After several minutes, she lay still and exhausted, and her thoughts wandered back to the night before last, when she and Del had confessed their love for each other.

His sweet words echoed through her mind—he had pledged his love to her, had sworn that she alone would have his love and devotion until the day he died. Drawing a shuddering breath, Ginny closed her eyes and reached down deep within herself, forcing herself to hold on to Del Harrigan's words. She made up her mind that she was going to believe him—and that the redheaded woman was lying. Besides, anyone looking at her could tell that Helen Coffman was not Del Harrigan's kind. He was a good, honest, and decent man . . . a man of God. With a sigh of resolve, Ginny decided that she would not believe what Helen Coffman had told her unless Del admitted it was so.

Her mind made up, the young schoolteacher got to her feet, looked around, and began cleaning the house, as if to clear away the doubts along with the cobwebs. And yet, despite her efforts, a gnawing little voice at the back of her mind kept telling her that Helen Coffman had spoken the truth. As Ginny mopped, swept, dusted, and washed windows, she prayed for Del Harrigan's quick and safe return. He was the only one who could settle her doubts forever.

*   *   *

It was early afternoon and Ginny Wheeler was on the front porch washing windows when four men—strangers to her—rode up and dismounted in front of her house. Eyeing them carefully, she noticed that one of the men was quite expensively dressed and well groomed. The other three were roughly clad and hard-edged. They remained slightly aloof as the dapper man stepped up on the porch, touched his hat, and said through an obsequious smile, "You are Mrs. Wheeler, I presume?"

Ginny stopped wiping the window, turned to face him squarely, and answered, "Yes, I'm Ginny Wheeler. What can I do for you?"

"My name is Perry Prince, ma'am," he explained. "I own the Silver Palace Saloon and Casino in Sioux City, and I need to talk to you about some business."

Ginny felt herself grow cold, remembering that Del Harrigan had told her it was Perry Prince's men who had chased Mack down and killed him. She thought quickly. She realized it would do her no good to reveal that she knew it was Prince's men who had killed her husband, as he would only deny any knowledge of it. Instead, she asked, "What is this business you speak of, Mr. Prince?"

The man smiled again and reached inside his coat, bringing out a brown envelope. Opening the flap, he produced several uniformly sized pieces of paper. "I received word of your husband's untimely death, Mrs. Wheeler," he told her, holding onto the papers, "and you have my condolences. However, his death has posed a rather serious difficulty for me." Fanning out the pieces of paper so Ginny could see the writing on them, he asked, "Do you recognize the signature on these, ma'am?"

Ginny nodded. "They are my late husband's."

"That is correct," he replied, still smiling. "Do you know what these are?"

"They look like IOUs to me."

"Correct again, ma'am. These IOUs total exactly five thousand dollars." The smile suddenly left his lips. "Since your husband isn't around to pay these off, I have come to collect it from you."

Ginny regarded him as coldly as he was regarding her. "Well, sir," she replied crustily, "you've made a long ride for nothing. I don't have five thousand dollars, or even a part of it. And if I did, you wouldn't get any of it. Those are Mack's debts, not mine. If you were foolish enough to extend him credit, that's your problem."

Prince's face darkened.

Ginny turned back to her window washing, saying over her shoulder, "I will thank you and your friends to kindly leave my property."

Prince did not comply. Stepping beside her, his eyes flashing with anger, he shook the papers in her face and growled, "I haven't ridden this far to be turned away by a smart-mouthed widow! These IOUs are legal debts that your late husband left behind—and believe me, I intend to collect!"

Ginny's own anger surfaced. Whipping around, she said bitingly, "I'm sure I know where Mack went, Mr. Prince. May I suggest you go there and collect it directly from him?"

The businessman's face grew redder. Through clenched teeth, Prince hissed, "You'd better honor this debt, lady. You can sell your house. I'll even let you sign a note for the balance so you can pay it off over time from your teacher's salary."

Ginny was of two minds. Annoyed that the man had known where to find her and what she did for a living, she was also fearful because she was no match for four men, and she did not know what they might do. Before she could respond, Prince threatened, "I'm going to collect my money from you, Mrs. Wheeler—one way or another!"

His words fueled her anger, and she lashed back, "You're not collecting one penny from me, mister! Now, get off my property, or I'll—"

"Or you'll what?" cut in Prince.

"What's going on here?" a familiar voice suddenly boomed from the street.

Ginny's heart bounded and she looked past Perry Prince to see Del Harrigan leaping off his horse. She watched him stride up her pathway, relieved that he was home safe and that he had come at this very opportune time.

"Del!" she cried, darting around Prince and running to him.

"You!" exclaimed Prince, immediately recognizing Harrigan.

"Yeah, me!" snapped the preacher. "I asked what's going on here!"

Prince began to explain, but Ginny cut him off and gave Harrigan the details herself. When she had finished, Harrigan eyed the four men heatedly and said, "Mack's debts were not his wife's debts. True, you lost five thousand dollars, Mr. Prince, but you can well afford it—far more than Mrs. Wheeler ever could. Now take your hirelings and get out of here!"

The saloon owner's men looked ready to tackle Harrigan, but Perry Prince lifted a hand to stay them. Holding his gaze on the tall, muscular man for a long moment, Prince told his cohorts, "Let's go, boys."

Ginny watched Harrigan's face as he glared at them until they had ridden out of sight. But when he put an arm around her shoulders, she felt suddenly uneasy.

Harrigan guided her toward the doorway, and as they entered the house, he told her, "I'm sure you heard that Fighting Bear came after us."

"Yes," she replied, her mind suddenly straying to the woman who was at that very moment lounging in Del's hotel room. "And I'm . . . I'm glad you're back safe."

"How about fixing me a cup of coffee, and I'll tell you what happened."

"All right," Ginny replied absently. "Sit down while I make it. I won't be long." Turning from him, she hurried into the kitchen, suddenly feeling far more fearful than she had while confronting Perry Prince and his henchmen.

137

Chapter Thirteen

Del Harrigan and Ginny Wheeler sat across from each other at the kitchen table, drinking their coffee, and the preacher related what had happened with Fighting Bear and the three killers. He concluded, "I've decided that I've got to ride out to the village and have a talk with Eagle Claw. And, as Fighting Bear said I should, I'm going to pray that the chief will understand that we couldn't control what those three no-goods did."

He glanced at Ginny, who was idly toying with the handle on her coffee cup, not looking at him.

He added, "I'm really wondering if Eagle Claw is going to be satisfied just to have those three in his hands. He's liable to—" Harrigan was suddenly aware that Ginny was not listening to him. "Darling," he breathed, reaching across the table and putting his hand on her arm, "did Prince and his men bother you that much?"

Ginny slowly lifted her eyes and looked at him. Her face was drawn and pale, and her usually bright eyes were dull. "No, Del," she replied, barely able to meet his gaze. "Prince didn't disturb me nearly as much as something else has."

Gently cupping her chin with his hand, he studied her face and asked, "What is it then, Ginny, dear?"

She seemed to be having trouble forming the words, for her mouth moved, but no sound emerged. Finally she blurted, "Do you know a woman named Helen Coffman?"

Ginny's eyes were riveted on Harrigan's face as he

138

stared blankly at her for a few seconds; then he remembered the flirty redhead who had ridden with him on the stagecoach. Nodding, he told her, "Yes. She's a card dealer at a saloon in Presho. She was a passenger on the stage with me for part of the trip. Why?"

Ginny drew a long shaky breath. "Well, she arrived in Red Buffalo yesterday on another stage—looking for you."

Harrigan felt his scalp tighten. "For me?"

Nodding glumly, Ginny explained, "She convinced Bernie Walker that the two of you are very close friends, and he let her stay in your room. She's there right now."

"Close friends?" he echoed incredulously.

"And according to her, it's deeper than that," Ginny continued. "I was so upset when Frank Meeker came and told me about it, that I went to the hotel and had a talk with her. I immediately told her that you and I are engaged, and . . . and she said something was fishy, because you and she had been lovers, and she's come here to marry you."

Harrigan felt a flush of anger begin at the base of his neck and work its way upward. "Why, of all the . . . Ginny, she's nothing but a cheap flirt—and a liar, to boot! I never laid eyes on her before she got on the stage, and I haven't seen her since. Something's fishy, all right—and the smell is coming from Helen Coffman!"

Ginny's lower lip began trembling, and she closed her eyes and put her hand over his, releasing a tremulous sigh. Harrigan stood up and went to her, folding her in his powerful arms. He realized what this had done to Ginny's confidence—and that her old wounds still brought her pain. Holding her tight, the preacher whispered, "Darling, I meant what I said the other night. I love you, and no other woman interests me—least of all a cheap, painted-up card dealer. You've got to believe me."

Ginny began to cry. Clinging to him, she sobbed, "I do believe you, Del, I do! It's just that—"

"I know. Mack's unfaithfulness." He kissed her tenderly, telling her, "All I can say is I hope it won't be too

139

much longer before you can put all that behind you forever—and know beyond a shadow of a doubt that you are safe with me, my dearest."

Ginny wept for several minutes. Slowly her crying subsided, and Harrigan kissed the top of her head and declared, "I'm going over to the hotel right now to put that woman in her place." Assuring Ginny once more that he loved only her, the preacher kissed her soundly, promised to come back as soon as he got Helen Coffman out of his room, and then hurried outside and mounted up.

After leaving his horse at Jimmy Boyd's stable, Del Harrigan headed for the hotel, and with every step he took, his anger grew. Striding through the hotel lobby, Harrigan noticed peripherally that Bernie Walker was not at the desk. He reached the staircase and stomped loudly up to the second floor. When he reached his room, he turned the doorknob, finding it unlocked, and stormed inside.

The redhead was standing before the dresser mirror, refreshing her makeup, and she smiled provocatively at his reflection. "Hello, sugar. I saw you coming up the street from the window—but, my goodness, you walk too fast. You didn't give me time to get all prettied up for you."

Looking from Helen to the two suitcases and the small bag sitting on the floor by the bed, Harrigan snapped, "What are you doing in my room?"

The woman turned around to face him. Fluttering her long eyelashes, she replied sweetly, "Why, honey, I didn't think you'd mind since we—"

"Since we *what*?"

"You know, darling," she said coyly, swaying toward him. "We never actually got to be alone, of course, but we both know what happened between us on that trip."

"*Nothing happened between us!*" he fumed, emphasizing each word.

Helen stopped abruptly three feet away from him, her face registering shock. She stared at him for a long moment and then said artfully, "What do you mean, nothing happened between us? What about the way we spoke to each other with our eyes? And . . . and the kiss we shared before we parted? And when I said I would see you again, you said, 'Sure thing.' Del, darling, I've lived for the moment we could be alone together. I simply don't understand."

"There's nothing to understand! You've got a vivid imagination, lady, that's all!" Harrigan growled. "If there was any talking with eyes going on in the coach, it was on your part, not mine. And when we parted in Presho, you kissed me—I did *not* kiss you. As for my saying you would see me again, I was just being polite." He glared at her, adding contemptuously, "I see with you that's a mistake."

Pain and surprise showed in Helen's eyes. "But darling," she protested, "I've come all this way just to be with you. I had wonderful plans for us."

"You had no business making plans for us!" Harrigan told her tartly. "And where did you get the gall to tell Ginny Wheeler that you and I were lovers and that we were going to be married?"

Helen did not answer his question. Instead, she stepped around him and pushed the door shut, and then forcibly embraced him. Looking at him through lowered lids, she insisted, "Kiss me, Del. There'll never be a woman who can make you as happy as I can."

Shoving her away, Harrigan said through clenched teeth, "You'll make me happy when you get out of this room and out of this town."

Fury engulfed the redhead, and her doll face went crimson. Baring her teeth, she hissed, "You'll be sorry for this, Del Harrigan! I quit a damn good job in Presho for a future with you—and I had it all worked out. You and I would be married and we'd be partners in your casino— why, with me dealing the cards, we couldn't miss. I happen to know some tricks with the deck that would've made us rich, and it wouldn't have been long till we owned a whole string of casinos. But now, you—"

"Hold it!" he blared. "Where on earth did you get the idea that I own a casino?"

"Well, anybody who knows anything can plainly see that you're a gambler. I just naturally assumed that you owned your own place—judging from the way you dress, you're obviously successful."

"You assumed a whole lot, Miss Coffman. It seems a man can't dress well without people thinking he's a gambler. Well, I'm not—and as a matter of fact, nothing could be further from reality. Do you want to know what I really am?"

"Well, I—"

"I am the pastor of the Red Buffalo Community Church! I'm a preacher, ma'am. A preacher of the Gospel!"

Helen buckled as though she had been kicked in the stomach. She stared at him in shock. "Y-you're a . . . a minister?"

"That's right. And furthermore, this minister is going to marry Ginny Wheeler. Now, would you be so kind as to leave this room? I've got to bathe and shave, and then meet my fiancée."

The redhead stood there, stunned, blinking her eyes repeatedly.

Opening the door, Harrigan said coldly, "I'll carry your bags down to the lobby for you."

Finding her voice, Helen answered, "Oh, you won't need to do that. I . . . I'll be taking a room until . . . until the next stage comes through. Just set them in the hall. I'll have the, uh, the clerk carry them to my room as soon as I register."

Picking up her bags, Harrigan set them in the hallway and closed the door behind Helen Coffman the moment she stepped out of his room.

Staring at the closed door, Helen felt that her whole world had just collapsed around her. She had been so certain that she had a future with gambler Del Harrigan. To be so rudely rebuffed and to learn that he was a preacher at the same time was too much for her. In a daze, she walked in the wrong direction down the hall, and she suddenly found herself at the rear of the building, looking down a staircase that she realized must lead to the alley. She stopped and took a deep, calming breath, and then turned and started back the other way.

Helen had taken only three steps when she noticed that the door of the room to her right was slightly ajar, and her mind started racing. Making sure no one else was in the hall, she peered into the room. It had been cleaned, and the bed was made up, but there were no signs that it was occupied. The maid had apparently forgotten to lock the door.

Her mind was crystal clear now, and a terrible scheme began to take shape. Smiling wickedly, she decided she would have her revenge on Del Harrigan and the woman he was planning to marry. If she could not have him, she would fix it so Ginny Wheeler would not want him. *While I'm at it*, she told herself, *I think I'll bring his ministry down too*.

She tiptoed back to where her luggage was sitting in the hallway, her anger giving her the strength to carry the cases to the unoccupied room in one trip. Setting them just inside the room, she caught her breath, and then walked back down the hall. Quickly descending the stairs, she was pleased to see that the desk clerk was on duty, and she smiled broadly at him.

Bernie Walker returned the smile and said, "Hello, Miss Coffman. Somebody told me the posse is back. I'm sure Reverend Harrigan will be showing up very soon."

"He already did," she giggled, adding confidentially, "It sure is wonderful to be in his arms again." Helen was delighted when the clerk's smile faded and puzzlement spread over his face. Leaving the clerk gaping at her, the redhead sashayed across the lobby and left the hotel.

For the rest of the afternoon, Helen Coffman walked about town, meeting people on the street and in the shops. She deliberately brought up Del Harrigan's name in conversation, asking people if they knew him. Whenever she received acknowledgment, Helen followed with, "He's a sweetheart, isn't he? I'm an old flame of his. We

143

haven't seen each other in some time, but when I found out he had moved here, I just had to come and see him." Every time she spun her tale, she was thrilled to get the expected response—obvious disbelief. Chuckling to herself, the redhead strolled around Red Buffalo, biding her time.

After washing up, Del Harrigan returned to Ginny Wheeler's house, anxious to tell her that he had sent Helen Coffman packing. When he arrived at her house, he found the young schoolteacher sitting on the front porch, watching for him. As he stepped up to her, he read the love in her eyes, and he knew her doubts had been relieved. Taking her in his arms, he assured her with a smile, "The woman has her own room until the next stage. There won't be any more trouble from her."

Ginny squeezed him tight and breathed, "Oh, Del, please forgive me for doubting you. I'm so sorry!"

"There's nothing to forgive. I completely understand, darling," he responded lightly. "Besides, everything is all right now."

Suddenly the thundering sound of galloping horses, punctuated with the war whoops of Indians, met their ears. The Indians were apparently on Main Street two blocks away, and the preacher's head whipped around in that direction. "You stay here!" he commanded Ginny, bounding off the porch.

Running after him, Ginny shouted, "Del! You're not wearing a gun!"

Ignoring Harrigan's protests, Ginny ran with him, and even before they rounded the first corner they could see smoke rising from the buildings along Main Street. Reaching the main thoroughfare, Harrigan was surprised to see that the Indians, whom he presumed had been Sioux, were already gone. They had apparently galloped through town, shooting flaming arrows into the buildings in the business district, and then ridden out almost before anyone could react. Now, however, the citizens of Red Buffalo were dashing about trying to put out the fires.

144

Bucket brigades were quickly set up, and men, women, and children worked together to try to douse the fires before they got out of control. Del Harrigan joined one of the brigade lines to help, and Ginny Wheeler got in line beside him.

The entire population of Red Buffalo labored frantically to save their town. Men took turns working the handles on the water pumps along Main Street while others dipped buckets into the troughs and kept the water moving to those who were throwing it on the flames.

It was nearing sundown when the last fire was doused. Eight buildings had been damaged, three of them severely enough to need major rebuilding. Fortunately for Del Harrigan, the Red Buffalo Hotel had suffered only minor damage to its front porch.

As the weary people gathered together in the center of town, they all were thankful that there had been only a slight breeze when the Indians came. If there had been a high wind, the town undoubtedly would have been burned to the ground.

Helen Coffman had observed the whole thing from an obscure spot between two buildings. Seeing Del Harrigan standing with the woman he loved firmed Helen's resolve, and she moved stealthily to the back of the hotel and climbed the stairs. Slipping into the unoccupied room, she sat in a chair with the door cracked open, positioning herself so that she had a clear view of room number twelve. With infinite patience, the redhead waited and watched for the preacher's return.

The Reverend Del Harrigan had unwittingly become Red Buffalo's leader, and the townspeople surrounded him, asking what they should do about the Indians. They greatly feared that such attacks would be repeated until the town was burned to the ground.

With Ginny Wheeler standing beside him, Harrigan gazed at their frightened faces and replied, "Well, I had already made up my mind to go to Eagle Claw and talk to him before this happened. I'll take Lone Fox's body to him, and make an apology for the whole town. With God's grace, maybe that will be enough to soothe his anger."

Touching his arm, Ginny said worriedly, "But Del, Eagle Claw is obviously furious. If you go to his village, what are the chances that he would torture and kill you?"

"It's a possibility," conceded Harrigan, "but I don't think there's really any choice in the matter—or if there *is* another solution, I haven't thought of it. I feel the responsibility for the apology is mine because I'm the one who told Eagle Claw that Lone Fox would be safe here. Now I can't just stand by and let him destroy my town."

Cal Stearns pushed his way through the crowd and declared, "Reverend, seeing as how you did such a fine job leading the posse, how about if you become Red Buffalo's marshal? We sure could use someone like you."

A murmur of assent went up from the crowd, but Harrigan merely smiled, shaking his head emphatically. "I appreciate your support—as well as your need for a new marshal—but my calling is to be a preacher, not a lawman, and I do not ever want to have to kill again if I can help it."

Standing in the crowd and listening, Frank Meeker suddenly had an idea—a last-ditch effort to win Ginny. If *he* became the town's marshal, the schoolteacher might be sufficiently impressed by his courage to forget Harrigan. Although the prospect of going up against hooligans and miscreants did not exactly excite him, he felt he had no alternative.

Stepping beside Harrigan, Meeker loudly announced, "Good people, I would like to volunteer to become Red Buffalo's marshal." He listened with satisfaction to the ripple of approval running through the crowd, and then added, "As long as I can continue to keep my job at the stage office, that is."

Being desperate for a lawman, the town councilmen—all present on the bucket brigade—hired him immediately.

Meeker threw a sidelong glance at Ginny. His heart sank when he realized that not only did she not seem to be impressed, she did not even seem to be aware of him. When she left with Del Harrigan, offering the preacher a hearty home-cooked meal, Frank Meeker felt his heart sink even lower. But he would not give up yet. Wearing the marshal's badge, and given a little more time, he might eventually sway her feelings.

At the same time that Del Harrigan was kissing Ginny Wheeler good night and assuring her that he would be careful when he went to the Sioux village the next morning, Helen Coffman was keeping vigil in the vacant room at the hotel. Growing drowsy and yawning repeatedly, she wished Harrigan would show up so she could put her sinister plan into action.

She yawned again some ten minutes later, but she stifled the yawn and sat up when she heard male voices down in the lobby. Her heart started pounding; she was sure one of the voices was Del Harrigan's. Moments later she saw Harrigan's tall, broad-shouldered form walking down the hallway to room number twelve. As soon as he entered the room and closed the door, Helen slipped out of her hiding place and stealthily made her way down the back stairs to the alley. Keeping to the wall of the hotel in the darkness, she crept toward the street, and when she reached the corner of the building, she paused and peered around the edge, making sure there was no one on the street to see her. Then she stepped onto the boardwalk and entered the lobby.

Frank Meeker was leaning on the desk in conversation with Bernie Walker, saying, "Well, now that I'm the new town marshal, I guess I'd better put the town to bed." He looked up at the clock on the wall. "The stage from Rapid City will be here at eight in the morning, and I've got some work to do before it gets here. So I'll make my rounds and—"

"Hello, gentlemen," Helen Coffman chirped as she glided across the lobby toward the staircase. The two men looked at her. Smiling warmly, she asked, "Reverend Harrigan did come in a few moments ago, didn't he?"

147

"Yes, ma'am," Walker assured her.

"Good. I told him I would be right behind him." She gave them an insinuating smile and said, "Good night."

Helen saw the two men eye each other with bewilderment as she started up the stairs. Then Walker called after her, "Won't you be needing a room for the night, Miss Coffman?"

Calling over her shoulder, she replied with a giggle, "I already have one, thank you."

Helen knew the two men could not see Harrigan's door from there, but she had exactly what she wanted from them. They would now be listening intently, straining to hear every sound.

Reaching Harrigan's door, Helen knocked on it, calling loudly, "Del, darling! It's Helen!"

The sound of a boot hitting the floor met Helen's ears. Then there was a pause, followed by the soft sound of stockinged feet padding across the floor. The door flew open and, keeping her voice low so that the men downstairs could not distinguish her words, she smiled and told the preacher, "I just wanted to tell you good-bye."

Harrigan's eyebrows arched. "Good-bye?"

"Yes, darling. Good-bye. If there's an empty seat on the stage tomorrow, I'll be on it. That is . . , ah . . unless you've changed your mind about marrying Ginny."

"Never," came the preacher's firm reply.

Looking sad, Helen sighed, "I thought so. Well, wish me luck. I'm returning to Presho to see if I can get my old job back."

"I'm sure you'll do fine," he told her stiffly. "Good bye." Then he shut the door in her face.

Helen stared at the door for a few seconds and then glanced back at the staircase. There was no one there. She hurriedly tiptoed to the empty room at the end of the hall and slipped back inside, closing and locking the door. Having heard that the preacher was intending to go to the Indian village at sunup, she planned to descend the stairs just before dawn, making it appear that she had been in Harrigan's room all night. If by some chance Harrigan

ught up to her before she left town, she would make a
ene and convince anyone listening that they had been
gether all night and were having a lovers' quarrel. If she
d not run into him, she would merely board the stage
d ride away. Either way, the damage would have been
ne, because the two men in the lobby would certainly
ll what they saw. Harrigan would undoubtedly lose his
ecious brunette, and he would surely lose his ministry.
e sneered, telling herself, *Nobody dumps little Helen
ke that and gets away with it*.

Frank Meeker finally pulled his eyes away from the
aircase and looked at Bernie Walker. "Tell me," he
ked the desk clerk, "do you still sleep on a cot there
hind the desk?"

"Sure do," answered Walker. "And I'm a light sleeper,
o." He smiled. "Don't worry. No matter when she comes
t of his room, I'll know about it."

"Good," Meeker declared, grinning maliciously. "Once
e can establish that she was with Harrigan all night, I'll
ve quite a story to tell to Ginny. See you in the morn-
g, Bernie."

Chapter Fourteen

After tossing and turning until nearly two o'clock in tl morning, Del Harrigan finally decided that since he cou. not sleep, he might just as well set out for the Siou village and arrive there by dawn. Rising from the bed, l quickly dressed and stepped out into the hallway ar down the stairs.

He walked quietly across the lobby, careful not awaken Bernie Walker, who was snoring loudly on the c behind the desk. Then he stepped outside into the co night air, passing no one on the dark street as he made h way to the stable. Knowing that the hostler, Jimmy Boy lived in a small room next to the livery office, Harriga made as little noise as possible when he went into tl corral, although his horse nickered a greeting as he a proached the animal in the pale moonlight.

"Hush, boy," the preacher whispered. "We don't wan to wake Jimmy up."

Disturbed by his presence, a couple of the oth horses in the corral whinnied nervously as he saddled ar bridled his mount, but they soon quieted down. Then l realized he would need a second horse to carry Lone Fox body to the Sioux village and, feeling certain that Jimm would not mind, bridled another horse.

The rusty hinges on the corral gate squealed ; Harrigan opened and closed it, and he smiled to himsel thinking how things always sounded their loudest whe one was trying to keep them their quietest. He led tl two animals to the street, where he mounted his bay, and rode toward the south end of town. At the partially built church, he dismounted and made his way to where Lone Fox's frail body lay hidden. He picked it up and carried it gently in his arms, draped it over the spare horse's back, and then headed northeastward toward the Sioux village.

Half lying in the chair she had placed directly in front of the window, Helen Coffman awakened when the first hint of light entered the room. She yawned and stretched, and then cautiously opened the door and looked out along the hallway. It was clear. Gambling that there would be room on the stagecoach, she picked up her two suitcases and her small bag and made her way to the staircase. As she started down, she decided that if the clerk was not yet awake, she would take care of that by letting a suitcase tumble from her hand directly in front of the desk. She had to be sure he would think she had spent the night with Del Harrigan.

Reaching the middle of the stairs, Helen was pleased to see that both the clerk and the new marshal were standing at the desk drinking coffee. She smiled at them, and Frank Meeker immediately dashed up the stairs, saying, "Here, ma'am, let me help you."

Meeker took the two suitcases to the bottom of the stairs. Helen thanked him and then, in a confiding tone, she half whispered, "I didn't want to awaken Del. He begged me not to leave yet, but I really must get on back home. Do you know if there's an available seat on this morning's stage from Rapid City?"

"There is, ma'am," Meeker assured her, setting the suitcases down. "According to the roster, there'll be only three people on board when it arrives—which will be in a couple of hours."

"Good," she sighed. Then, smiling coyly, she patted her hair and exclaimed, "I must look a mess! May I use the facilities at the Butterfield office to freshen up, Mr. Meeker? Like I told you, I didn't want to awaken Del."

"Yes, ma'am," replied Meeker. "I'll carry your suitcases down there right now and open up the place for you."

"Oh, thank you," Helen breathed, "you're so very kind. I guess I'd better get some breakfast after I freshen up." Pausing deliberately, she looked at the two men, and then lowered her eyes. "For, uh, Del's sake, perhaps it would be best if you didn't, uh, mention to anyone that I spent the night in his room. You know . . . him being a minister and all."

She was pleased to see Walker and Meeker eye each other furtively. She knew there would be plenty to tell—and they would tell it. But Meeker nodded knowingly and assured her, "We understand, ma'am. Now, let me carry your bags."

As soon as Frank Meeker had taken Helen Coffman to the Butterfield office, leaving her to tend to her grooming, he ran back to the hotel. He wanted to tell Ginny Wheeler what he knew as soon as possible—but he also wanted to take Bernie Walker with him to verify his story. Reaching the hotel, he dashed into the lobby, almost skidding into the desk in his haste.

"Bernie," he puffed, "I want you to go with me to Ginny's house right now."

Walker's brow puckered. "What for?"

"I need your word to back up mine—and I want to go now, before Harrigan gets up. She needs to know that he's playing her for a fool, and he may have planned to see her before he heads out to talk to Eagle Claw."

"But she's probably still asleep," argued Walker.

"Then we'll wake her up. She's got to know—and she has a right to know immediately."

Sighing, Bernie Walker followed Frank Meeker through the streets of Red Buffalo. It took several minutes to awaken Ginny, but Frank Meeker knocked persistently on her door until he heard her approaching footsteps.

The sleepy-looking brunette opened the door part way, blinking against the light of the rising sun. Meeker

hought how beautiful she was, even when she had just
wakened.

Looking slightly annoyed at this early intrusion, she
sked, "What is it?"

"I need to talk to you, Ginny," Meeker insisted.

"I only got to sleep a couple of hours ago," she told
im tartly.

Looking at Walker and then at Ginny again, Meeker
xplained, "I've got something very important to tell you,
therwise I wouldn't have awakened you." He paused for
ffect and then continued, "You're not going to like it, but
t's the truth, and I brought Bernie with me to corroborate
t."

Ginny tightened the sash on her robe and swung the
door wide. "All right," she sighed, "come in." When they
ntered the house, she closed the door, made a gesture
or them to be seated in the parlor and then sat down
acing them. Rubbing her eyes, she asked wearily, "Now
vhat's this bad news?"

Trying to keep the pleasure he was feeling off his
ace, Meeker blurted, "Your friend Reverend Harrigan
ust spent the night with Helen Coffman."

Ginny's eyes flashed, and she suddenly seemed wide
wake. "What are you talking about?"

Meeker told her everything he had seen and heard,
nd Walker assured her that the stationmaster was telling
he truth.

Ginny blinked in disbelief, putting a shaky hand to
her throat. "No," she mumbled. "It just can't be. It just
an't be. She's lying! Maybe she just pretended to go up
o his room. Maybe she spent the night elsewhere, then
nade it look like she'd been with Del."

"Elsewhere?" chuckled Walker. He shook his head.
"I'm sorry, Mrs. Wheeler, but I'm the man who rents out
he rooms, and I'm telling you she was in room twelve all
night with the reverend."

Meeker saw Ginny's pain on her face. Moving beside
her, he took hold of her hands and said soothingly, "I
knew it was going to hurt you, dearest, but it's better that

you find out now than to let yourself fall in love with him and then learn that he's a womanizing hypocrite."

Ginny Wheeler tried to speak, but the words would not come. Looking agitated, she stood, but her legs would not support her. Meeker jumped up and took her in his arms as she stared blankly and then broke into wordless sobbing. Bernie Walker, looking embarrassed as well as saddened, silently took his leave.

Frank Meeker waited until the door had closed behind the hotel clerk, and then, holding the schoolteacher close, he whispered in her ear, "I love you, Ginny. And promise that if you'll give me the chance to be your husband, I will always be true to you—always."

Perry Prince paced impatiently in the kitchen of the abandoned farmhouse where he and his henchmen had holed up. As his men awakened one by one, Prince decided bitterly that he was not through with Ginny Wheeler —or with Del Harrigan—by a long shot. If he was not going to get his money, at least he would have the satisfaction of killing them both.

The light of the rising sun filtered through the grimy windows of the old house, and the men sat on the floor and ate a breakfast of hardtack, beef jerky, and whiskey Facing Roger Gann, Neal Palmer, and Jack Beemer, Prince said, "All right, men, let's go over the plan again. We'll return to Red Buffalo and kidnap that acid-mouthed widow and bring her to this house. We'll use her to lure Harrigan out here—and then we'll kill them both." He looked from man to man. "Any questions?"

The three men looked at each other and then back at Prince, shaking their heads.

"Okay," Prince said, standing, "let's not waste any more time. Let's ride."

The four men had started toward the door when Jack Beemer, the oldest of the bunch, suddenly clutched his chest and paled, leaning against the door frame. Peering at his face, Prince asked, "What's the matter, Jack?"

"I dunno, Perry. I'm feelin' kinda sick. Give me a coupla of minutes, will ya?"

But Prince was feeling too impatient. Shaking his head, he told his cohort, "No, you just wait here for us. It won't take all four of us to grab that one little woman anyway. Don't worry about it, Jack. You just rest some more."

Moments later, the three men mounted up and rode hard for Red Buffalo.

A broken-hearted Ginny Wheeler sat in her parlor and stared through the open window, seeing nothing. She had been relieved when Frank Meeker left to meet the incoming Rapid City stage that was due to depart again at nine o'clock. The old grandfather clock in the corner was now chiming nine bells, but Ginny's mind had drifted off, and she barely heard it.

Instead, she listened to the contented humming coming from next door and sadly wondered if *she* would ever feel happy again. When she had opened her windows earlier to let the cool morning breeze in, she had noticed her neighbor's seventeen-year-old son, Kent Early, sitting on the back porch, cleaning his double-barreled shotgun. One of her favorite students, Kent would graduate next spring. Ginny had briefly thought about going over and speaking with him to distract herself, but with her eyes red and swollen, she decided against it.

Her tortured mind settled once again on Del Harrigan. How could he be so cruel as to toy with her emotions, knowing how she had suffered because of Mack's infidelity? Not only that—how could he be such a bald-faced hypocrite? That was the worst thing of all! Standing in the pulpit with a Bible in his hand, pretending that he was a man of God, and all the while . . .

Gritting her teeth, Ginny tried to hate him. But she still loved him, and try as she might to cast off the love and replace it with hate, she could not do it. Angry at herself, she decided that it would take time, but she was determined to do it. *It'll help a lot,* she thought, *when I can look him right in the eye and tell him what I think of him!*

Then Ginny remembered the mission that Harrigan had undertaken. Maybe he would never return, and he would never learn what she was feeling. Maybe Eagle Claw would rob her of that pleasure by killing him. Maybe—

Suddenly her attention was drawn to the middle of the street and the three men guiding their horses toward her house. She recognized them immediately. It was Perry Prince and two of his henchmen. Ginny's jaw tightened, and a cold ripple of fear ran down her spine. Prince and his men were up to no good—and it showed clearly on their faces.

Frightened, the schoolteacher dashed to a desk drawer and pulled out her dead husband's Colt .45 revolver. Breaking it open, she checked to see if it was loaded and then snapped it shut and thumbed back the hammer. She felt the sweat beading on her brow, and the palms of her hands were moist. Wiping her hands on her apron, she gripped the gun firmly in both hands and went to confront her adversaries.

Perry Prince was two strides ahead of his men as they stepped onto the porch. They were taken completely by surprise when Ginny, her eyes blazing, bolted through the front door, holding the revolver on them. "Get those hands in the air!" she barked. "I mean right now!"

Prince's two cohorts started to go for their guns, but Ginny pointed the Colt .45 between their leader's eyes and blared, "Touch those guns and your boss dies!"

The henchmen checked themselves and looked at Prince questioningly. It was Prince's turn to sweat as he looked down the barrel of the quivering revolver. Lifting his hands very slowly, he splayed them and said evenly, "Now, take it easy, Mrs. Wheeler. We're not here to cause you any trouble. We're just here to—"

"To what?" she demanded. Then, answering her own question, she spat, "To wring my money out of me, right?"

Before Prince could answer, Ginny screamed loudly, "Kent! Kent! Bring your shotgun and come here!"

Seconds later, the seventeen-year-old youth rounded the corner of Ginny's house, shotgun in hand. When he saw his teacher holding the gun on three strange men, he pulled back the hammers and lined the twin barrels on them. "What's going on, Mrs. Wheeler?" he asked.

"These men were here to rob me, Kent," she replied hotly, glaring at Perry Prince.

"We were doing nothing of the kind!" Prince exclaimed defensively. "We just wanted to talk to you."

While Ginny refuted his words, two men rode by in a wagon, and Kent hailed them for help. The men quickly assisted the schoolteacher, disarming the three culprits and taking them to the office of Marshal Frank Meeker.

Following them to the jail, Ginny repeated her story to the marshal. Prince loudly insisted that he and his men had committed no crime, but Meeker, eager to make strides with Ginny, locked them up, telling them that he would hold them until the circuit judge came around—which would be in about six weeks. Leaving the three men to swear at him through the bars, Frank Meeker then escorted Ginny Wheeler back to her home.

On the road heading east, Helen Coffman laid her head against the seat back and watched the passing landscape through the stagecoach window. In a brief conversation with Frank Meeker just before she boarded the stage, she discovered that he had indeed told the story to Ginny Wheeler, and that the little schoolmarm's romance with Del Harrigan was over. Helen had no doubt that the story would spread quickly through the small town, and when that happened, Del Harrigan would also be finished as pastor of the Red Buffalo Community Church.

Smug in her victory, the redhead smiled. *It's just like they say, Mr. Harrigan,* she thought to herself. *Hell hath no fury like a woman scorned. Let that be a lesson to you.*

Del Harrigan sat on his horse and peered at the Indian village that lay along the banks of a winding creek a quarter mile away. He could see people milling about,

and cookfires were burning—and he knew that if he coul
see the villagers, the sentries had no doubt spotted him
Nudging his mount, he moved slowly toward the encamp
ment, and when he was within two hundred yards, Ind
ans suddenly rose up as if springing out of the ground an
surrounded him. All of them carried rifles.

Lifting his hand in the sign of peace, he told them, "
am unarmed. I come in peace to talk with your chie
Eagle Claw."

Two of them stepped up to the horse that bore Lon
Fox's body and eyed the corpse.

"I have brought Lone Fox to you," Harrigan ex
plained, "so you could give him a proper burial."

The warriors grunted and escorted him to the cente
of the village, telling him to wait while they relayed new
of his arrival to Fighting Bear.

Summoned from his tepee, the war chief was stern a
he told the preacher to get off his horse. As Harriga
dismounted, Fighting Bear commanded several of the brave
to take Lone Fox's body and prepare it for burial.

Meeting the Sioux warrior's hard gaze, Harrigan tol
him, "I would like to talk to Eagle Claw now."

Fighting Bear's eyes seemed to burn into the minis
ter, and he replied stiffly, "You wait here, preacher man.
Leaving a passel of braves surrounding Harrigan, h
wheeled and walked toward a large tepee directly in th
center of the village.

Only a few moments had passed when the war chie
emerged from the large tepee. His expression and voic
giving nothing away, he told Harrigan, "Chief Eagle Cla
thanks you for returning Lone Fox to his people. Eagl
Claw will have powwow with preacher man after buria
ceremony."

Del Harrigan was then escorted to an empty tepe
and told to wait inside. He was further ordered by Figh
ing Bear to remain there until Eagle Claw was ready t
see him, with the warning that it was against tribal custor
to allow white men to observe burial ceremonies. The wa

chief again left well-armed warriors on guard to ensure that his command was carried out.

Harrigan sat down on the ground inside the tepee, listening as drums began to beat and a mournful chant was taken up by the entire village. The dirge seemed to go on for hours, and time moved slowly for the minister. The shadows shifted inside the tepee, and finally, sometime in midafternoon, the drums went quiet and the chanting stopped. About a half hour later, Fighting Bear came for Harrigan and escorted him to the chief's tepee.

Pulling back the tent flap, the war chief told Harrigan to enter. He found Eagle Claw alone in the tepee, sitting cross-legged on a colorful blanket. The chief motioned for the white man to sit down in front of him and then asked in his deep bass voice, "Preacher man wanted powwow with Eagle Claw?"

"Yes, Chief," Harrigan confirmed. "I wish to explain to you how those three terrible men were able to capture and kill Lone Fox without my knowledge."

"Those men are dead," grunted the chief, and for the first time his face took on an expression—the hint of a smile.

"They had it coming," responded the preacher, wondering how severely the killers had been tortured before they died. Then, looking Eagle Claw square in the eye, he explained, "I have come on a mission of peace, Chief, to ask if it is possible for us to once again have harmony." He paused for a moment and then continued, "You have good reason to be angry, and I suppose deep in my heart I cannot blame you for sending your braves with flaming arrows to burn our town. I had told you Lone Fox would be safe, yet white men murdered him. But now I have come as representative of all the people of Red Buffalo to apologize for Lone Fox's death and to assure you that we do not wish any harm to you or your people."

There was respect in Eagle Claw's eyes for the forthright preacher. "You are a brave man," he stated simply. "I could torture you and kill you like those other three."

"I know I am at your mercy, Chief," Harrigan confessed, nodding, "but I truly want to be your friend. This is my way of showing you that I am sincere and want to be at peace with you and your people."

By his simple but eloquent words, Del Harrigan convinced the Sioux chief that the citizens of Red Buffalo were not his enemies, and Eagle Claw accepted Harrigan's hand of friendship, promising that there would be no more attacks on the town. The chief invited the preacher to stay and celebrate their newly formed bond, but, eager to make his report to the townspeople, Harrigan graciously declined and immediately mounted his horse and rode toward Red Buffalo. Feeling refreshed in spirit as well as body, he did not mind at all the strong northerly wind that buffeted him as he headed for home.

It was at sunset that Jack Beemer, concerned that Perry Prince and the other two men had not yet returned to the old farmhouse, rode into Red Buffalo. Asking questions along the street, he soon learned that Marshal Meeker had locked three men up in the jail—and from their descriptions, Beemer was sure it had been Prince, Gann, and Palmer. Knowing that Meeker would have no reason to lock him up, he went to the marshal's office to see if he could visit his friends. He found that the marshal was not there, but the door to the cell area was locked, and there were no keys in sight. Standing against the door, he called, "It's Jack! Is that you and the boys in there, Perry?"

"Yeah!" called Prince. "Come around to the back of the jail—there's a window we can talk through!"

Prince was waiting for Beemer at the cell window, which was covered with a heavy wire mesh so that no weapons could be passed inside.

Peering through the mesh, Prince gave his man a quick explanation as to how they had landed in the jail, and then told him, "We've got to get out of here, Jack. Now listen, you'll have to kidnap that Wheeler woman by yourself. As soon as it's dark enough, go to her house, gag her good, and take her out to the old farmhouse. Tie her up tight and then come back to town and find Harrigan.

Tell him there's another man with us and that he's got the Wheeler woman in a place where Harrigan will never find her. Say that if we aren't let out of jail so we can show up there within two hours, the man has instructions to kill her—so if Harrigan wants to see her alive again, he'd better get us out of here. Got it?"

"Got it, Perry," said Beemer. "I'll have you outta here soon. You just hold on."

He went around to the front of the building where he had tied his horse to the hitch rail and was about to mount up when he remembered seeing a pair of handcuffs lying on the desk. Looking around to make sure no one was watching, he hurried into the marshal's office, grabbed the handcuffs, and stuffed them in a pocket. He smiled to himself as he stepped back outside and untied his horse. Then, realizing he had some time to kill, he went to one of the saloons to wait for darkness to come.

Chapter Fifteen

The purple twilight was fading into darkness as Ginny Wheeler paced her kitchen floor. The young woman had never experienced such mixed emotions in all her life. Anger boiled inside her at Del Harrigan, who had so wickedly played her for a fool . . . yet she now feared for his life because he had not returned from the Sioux village. He should have been back hours ago. Wringing her hands and clenching them into fists as she paced the floor, Ginny asked herself how she could still care about Harrigan after what he had done. Yet, she had to admit to herself that as angry as she was, she still deeply loved him.

Ginny's pacing halted abruptly when she heard a knock at the front door. Her heart leaped in her breast. It had to be Harrigan! He would have no idea that she had learned of his night with Helen Coffman. Swallowing hard and bracing herself, Ginny hurried through the house to the front door and pulled it open. She found herself staring into the muzzle of a cocked revolver, and she instantly recognized one of Perry Prince's men from the first time he had come to her house.

"Don't give me a hard time, lady," snarled Jack Beemer. "You're comin' with me."

Ginny had no choice but to follow the man's orders, and moments later she was sitting in Beemer's saddle while he rode behind her, the muzzle of his gun poking her in the back.

"Okay, lady," he growled, "we're goin' for a little ride

162

ut to an old farmhouse. You open your mouth and I'll
last you! Got that?"

"Yes," she answered shakily, "but I don't understand
vhy."

He laughed sharply. "You're gonna be Perry's ticket
utta that stinkin' jail, that's why. You got him in there—
ow you're gonna get him out."

"How am I going to do that?" she asked as they rode
hrough the gathering darkness.

"Soon as I get you all nice and settled, I'm gonna find
our boyfriend and tell him unless he pulls some strings
vith the marshal and springs my pals, you'll die. Simple as
hat."

A wagon approached, and Beemer pressed the muz-
le of his gun hard against Ginny's ribs, whispering harshly,
One peep and you're dead!"

Ginny remained silent. When the wagon had passed,
he felt the kidnapper relax, and he spurred his horse as
hey neared the edge of town. Suddenly Beemer seemed
o tense again and he slowed the horse down. She found
erself wondering why and, as if reading her mind, he
old her, "I don't see no reason to ride all the way out to
he farmhouse just to have to turn around and come right
ack to find your boyfriend." He looked around, then
sked, "You're the schoolmarm, right?"

"Yes, that's right."

"Where's the schoolhouse?"

"On the south edge of town. Why?"

Wheeling the horse around, Beemer said, " 'Cause
hat's where we're goin' now. Show me where it is."

Ten minutes later, Ginny was being forced into the
choolhouse. Lighting a lamp and turning it down low,
Beemer set it on the floor near the huge cast-iron stove
nd then pulled the handcuffs he had taken from the
narshal's office from his hip pocket. Waving his gun at
er, Beemer ordered, "Okay, lady. On the floor."

"What are you doing?" she asked.

"I'm gonna handcuff you to this here stove. Ain't no

way you're gonna get loose from it while I'm out lookin
for your boyfriend."

The thick legs of the big potbellied stove were only
five inches high, and the young schoolteacher had to lie
flat on her back in order for Beemer to shackle her to it.
As the cuffs closed around her wrists, Ginny asked, "Do
you have the key to these handcuffs?"

"Nope," he answered dryly.

"How are you going to get me loose?"

"Won't need to, lady. The marshal can do that after
me and Perry and the boys are ridin' free across the
plains." Suddenly Beemer stiffened and rubbed at his
chest, obviously in pain. After a moment or two he shook
his head, as if to clear it, and then queried, "Okay, lady
where can I find your boyfriend?"

Ginny was afraid that no one might ever find Del
Harrigan again, but she said only, "He lives at the hotel
on Main Street."

"Which one?"

"There is only one. The Red Buffalo."

Kneeling down beside her, Beemer looked at her
dress and asked, "You got a handkerchief on you?"

"No. Why?"

Without answering, Beemer untied the linen kerchief
she had draped around her neck and whipped it off.
Twirling the large square between his two hands, he told
her, "I've gotta gag you so's you don't holler and get
somebody in here while I'm gone."

Ginny started to protest, but her words were muffled
as he roughly shoved the cloth between her teeth and
lifted her head enough to knot it tightly at the back. That
done, Beemer turned out the lamp and left, saying he
would see her later.

Feeling completely helpless, Ginny Wheeler wondered how long she would have to lie on the floor with her
hands cuffed around the leg of the huge stove before the
kidnapper accomplished his mission. One thing was for
sure: The man was right. There was no way she was going
to get loose.

*   *   *

It had been dark for about an hour when Del Harrigan drew within a few miles of Red Buffalo. Sporadic heat lightning split the sky, and the wind lashed at him with gusts so powerful that he had given up trying to keep his hat on his head, and instead rolled it up and tied it to the back of his saddle. The two horses kept trying to turn their rumps in the direction of the wind, but he managed to keep them headed for town.

The preacher had ridden another couple of miles when light from the north caught his attention again. Only this time it was not heat lightning that illuminated the night sky with such a startling glow. Pulling rein, he stood up in the stirrups and squinted against the wind with mounting horror. There was no question about it. A grass fire had set the prairie ablaze and the north wind was driving it straight toward Red Buffalo. His heart pounding, he studied the rolling wall of fire, estimating that at the rate it was moving, it would envelop the town in less than an hour. Harrigan let go of the reins of the animal he was leading. Spurring his horse's flanks, he sent it into a full gallop and raced for home.

Jack Beemer returned to the schoolhouse within twenty minutes. Slipping through the door, he did not bother to light the lamp but moved through the darkness toward the middle of the room where Ginny Wheeler lay on the floor, growing numb from her uncomfortable position.

Sitting down at a student's desk, he sighed and said sully, "Well, lady, looks like we may be in for a long night. Fella at the hotel said your Reverend Harrigan was on some kind of mission, and he didn't know when he might get back. I'll go check again a little later." So saying, he put his head down on the desk and fell asleep.

Ginny tried to keep her mind occupied while the henchman slept, convincing herself as best she could that no harm would come to her and she would soon be free. Staring up at the windows from her place on the floor, she was perplexed when she realized that instead of getting

165

darker, it was growing lighter. A cold shiver of fear ran down her spine as she realized that the light was really a glow—the glow from an enormous fire!

She began pounding the floor with her heels, trying to awaken the sleeping man. When Beemer sat up with a start, he looked over at the clock on the wall—apparently not even wondering how there could be light enough to read it by—and then declared, "I'll be damned. I slept over an hour. Well," he said, standing up and stretching, "I guess I'll go look for your boyfriend again." He turned to leave without looking at the young schoolteacher.

Whining desperately, Ginny finally got his attention. Beemer turned and stared at her curiously, as though trying to figure out what she was trying to tell him. Finally he told her, "Lady, if you're askin' me to let you go, forget it. I already told you I won't—and besides, since I don't have the key to them cuffs, even if I wanted to, there ain't no way I could."

Ginny's agitation increased, and, sighing, he went to her and bent down, pulling the gag out of her mouth so she could speak.

"Go look outside!" she screamed.

Looking perplexed, Beemer stood up and headed for the side door. He had obviously heard the excited voices and the rattle of wagons coming from the road—along with the howl of the wind—and he wheeled around and said, "I ain't openin' that door unless you're gagged."

With the handkerchief firmly in Ginny's mouth once more, the man walked back to the door and pushed it open, and a bright orange light shone on his face.

Jack Beemer's eyes bulged as he shouted, "Oh, my God, it's a fire! The whole sky's lit up! Damn, I've gotta get outta here!"

He started to dash outside when Ginny's terrified keening stopped him. He stood framed in silhouette in the doorway, staring at the helpless woman while she struggled frantically against the handcuffs. Beemer moistened his lips, looked outside at his horse, then faced Ginny again. "Aw, jeez, lady, there's nothin' I can do! Ain't no way I can lift that stove to get you loose. It probably weighs more'n three hundred pounds." He threw his hands helplessly into the air. "I'm sorry, but I got to save myself."

Ginny's breath seemed to lock in her lungs. She tried to cry out for Beemer to do something to save her, but she could only make a high-pitched whine.

Pivoting, Beemer took a step toward the door and abruptly stopped, clutching his chest. Then he staggered slightly and his knees buckled, and he slumped heavily across the threshold. Jack Beemer was dead.

A gust of wind hit the door, swinging it hard against Beemer's lifeless body. The door rebounded against the outside wall, then slammed against the corpse again. Ginny Wheeler's blood seemed to freeze in her veins as, completely helpless, she lay watching the deadly light grow ever brighter.

Thundering into Red Buffalo, Harrigan found the terrified townspeople packing their possessions into buggies and buckboards, getting ready to escape the rolling wall of flame that was bearing down on their town. Some people were already charging toward the White River, their aim being to cross the shallow stretch of water and wait in safety on the south bank.

The preacher's first concern was Ginny Wheeler, and he headed for her house. Guiding his mount close to the boardwalk to keep from colliding with careening vehicles, he pressed toward the side street that would take him there. At the same time, his eyes searched both sides of the street in case she was already fleeing.

Suddenly someone was tugging at Harrigan's leg and shouting above the din, "Preacher! Preacher!"

Pulling rein, he looked down into the face of deacon Harry Ronders.

"I'm glad you're back in one piece!" yelled Ronders. "Go around the corner at the end of the block! I need to talk to you and you won't be able to hear me over this noise!"

Ronders ran down the boardwalk, bumping into people as he went, and he was waiting for Harrigan when the preacher pulled his horse around the corner. As Harrigan dismounted quickly, he asked, "Harry, where's your family?"

"They're already across the river," said Ronders. "I came back to get as much of my stuff out of the shop as I could, and I happened to see you through the window."

"Have you seen Ginny?"

"No."

Turning back to his horse, Harrigan told the deacon, "I'll see you on the other side of the river. I've got to make sure she's all right."

Ronders's hand clamped down on Harrigan's arm. "Preacher, there's something you've got to know!" he declared.

"It'll have to wait, Harry," the tall man said, raising his foot toward the stirrup.

"But you've got to know this before you see Ginny!" Ronders shouted urgently.

Harrigan turned and faced him. "Make it quick," he insisted. "Time's running out."

While the wind howled and the noise of rattling vehicles and shouting people assaulted their ears, Harry Ronders told Del Harrigan the story that had raced through Red Buffalo as fast as a prairie fire about Helen Coffman and their alleged night together. The words hit Harrigan like a punch in the stomach, and he suddenly felt sick. His face paled as he said, "I suppose since Frank Meeker was the first one to talk with that scheming redhead, Ginny has learned about it, too."

"I'm sure she has," Ronders agreed.

Feeling even sicker, Harrigan looked searchingly at his deacon and asked, "Do *you* believe it, Harry?"

Ronders emphatically shook his head. "No," he said flatly, "I don't."

Harrigan laid a hand on the deacon's shoulder. "Thank you," he breathed, trying to smile. "I don't know how that woman made it look so genuine, but, Harry, I promise you before God that it's all a lie. I may never be able to prove it, but it's all a lie."

168

Ronders smiled and assured the preacher, "You don't have to prove it to me. Your word is good enough." Frowning, he continued, "You'd be hard-pressed to shake the truth out of Miss Coffman, though. She left town on the stage this morning."

Harrigan shook his head in amazement. "There's a name for her," he said through his teeth, "but I won't lower myself to use it." Eyes blazing, he hopped into the saddle. "I'd better find Ginny and tell her the truth—and hope that she believes me as easily as you do."

He spurred his horse and raced as fast as he could through the congested streets toward Ginny's house. Casting a glance toward the north, he saw the sky glowing red. Though he could not see the wall of fire, he knew it was getting closer.

As he neared Ginny's house, Harrigan saw Frank Meeker stepping off the porch. Skidding his horse to a stop, Harrigan asked, "Is she in there?"

"No," replied Meeker, looking worried, "and I don't know where she is. I've looked all over for her. No one else has seen her, either." The new marshal started to hurry away, explaining, "I've got to get back to the jail. That Perry Prince and his men showed up at Ginny's house this morning and threatened her, but fortunately, she called for help, and we got them safely locked up. Now, though, I've got to get them out before the fire hits."

Without speaking, Harrigan wheeled his horse around and headed for the jail himself. Moments later he stormed into the marshal's office and found the door to the cell area locked. His adrenaline flowing, he backed up a few steps and then hit the door hard with his shoulder, and splinters flew as the door burst open. He found Prince and his two henchmen standing at the cell window.

He looked at their expectant faces and hissed through his teeth, "Where is she, Prince?"

"What's going on out there?" asked the saloon owner as if Harrigan had not spoken.

"Prairie fire," replied the preacher tonelessly. "I asked you where Ginny Wheeler is."

An arrogant sneer curled Prince's upper lip. "My other man has her. I won't tell you where until I have five thousand dollars in my hands and my men and I are out of this two-bit jail."

The fire that ignited inside Del Harrigan was as hot as the one bearing down on Red Buffalo. Gritting his teeth, he rasped, "There's a sea of fire rolling toward this town in front of a high wind, Prince. The noise you're hearing out there is the people getting out of town and heading for the river. Now, you tell me where your man has Ginny, or so help me, I'll leave you right here to burn—just before the fires of Hell consume your souls."

Prince threw his head back and laughed. "That's not likely, is it? I understand you're a preacher, and leaving us here to burn to death when you could let us out would be murder." He smiled insolently, shaking his head. "No, you're not going to do that. Like I said, you'll find out where your sweetie is when I've got five thousand dollars in my hand and we're somewhere safe."

In disgust, Harrigan returned to the street and mounted his horse. He was trying to figure out what to do when he spotted Frank Meeker coming toward the jail. Heedlessly plunging his horse across the street in front of charging vehicles, he hauled up in front of Meeker and shouted, "Handcuff your prisoners together when you move them from the cell and don't let them out of your sight! Prince claims he's got Ginny hidden somewhere, that another of his men kidnapped her, and I've got to find her!" Without waiting for a response from the startled marshal, Harrigan galloped away.

Momentarily staring after Harrigan's retreating back, Frank Meeker began running after the preacher to join in the search for Ginny Wheeler. But then he stopped, saying aloud, "No, I can't. My first obligation is to the office of marshal." He angrily drove his fist into his palm, mumbling, "If it were up to me personally, those prisoners

170

could burn there for all I care—but as marshal of Red Buffalo, I guess I have to get them to safety."

He whirled around and ran along the boardwalk toward the jail, which was on the opposite side of the street. He stood waiting at the edge of the street for a break in the traffic, but buckboards and riders were barreling down the street in panic, desperate to flee the dreaded fire.

A minute passed, then two. Horses and horse-drawn wagons were racing along Main Street one after the other, allowing Meeker no opportunity to make a dash for the other side. Finally, in desperation, he picked what appeared to be a gap between two wagons and bolted into the street. At the same instant, a buckboard came careening around the corner from the side street. The driver did not see Meeker, nor did Meeker see the wagon before the tail end of it struck him, knocking him down. Dazed, he struggled to his feet only to be struck by a terrified, riderless horse.

A man in another wagon saw Meeker go down, and he yanked back on his reins, bringing his vehicle to a squealing halt. While other wagons and riders rushed past him, he leaped to the ground and knelt beside the unconscious marshal. Gathering Meeker up in his arms, the man laid him in the bed of the wagon amid various household articles, climbed back onto the seat, and sped away.

The Reverend Del Harrigan frantically raced about, asking anyone who would stop long enough to speak with him if they had seen Ginny Wheeler—but the answer was always no. In growing desperation, he continued searching for the schoolteacher, his attention constantly drawn toward the massive wall of flame that was bearing down on the town. It was stampeding with the swiftness of the fierce wind that was driving it and, true to its Indian name, the roaring blaze sounded like a thundering herd of buffalo.

Harrigan decided to take one more look in Ginny's house, realizing that all he had was Frank Meeker's word that she was not there. Perhaps Prince's man had left her tied up in a closet.

He led his horse onto her front lawn, stopping just before the house, and leaped onto the porch. Anxiously searching the house and finding nothing, he returned to his horse and galloped back to Main Street. It seemed that the entire town had been evacuated; Main Street was completely deserted.

The racing wall of fire reached the northern edge of Red Buffalo, and his horse began to snort and dance about. The noise was so deafening that even had he been aware of them, Harrigan could not have heard the screams of the three men who were still locked up in the jail.

The buildings at that end of town began bursting into flame, and the intense heat started peeling the paint off the walls of other buildings in the fire's path. Harrigan knew he had to get out of town immediately, and he tried to console himself with the hope that the man who had taken Ginny would have taken her to some safe place so as not to be trapped by the flames himself.

Galloping southward, the preacher's heart sank when he reached the partially built church, knowing it would soon be nothing but ashes. Suddenly his attention was drawn to the schoolhouse. Squinting, he watched the side door swinging in the wind, banging repeatedly against the wall, and although he could not make out what it was, there seemed to be something lying across the threshold. He realized that stopping to investigate now might mean the difference between life and death, but at the same time he sensed that something was amiss here.

Guiding his protesting horse over to the building, he leaped from his saddle and ran to the door. The form was a body, and one that he immediately recognized: Perry Prince's henchman. Stepping over the body, Harrigan raced into the room. In the glow of the fire, he could see Ginny writhing against her shackles, eyes wild and face glistening with sweat.

Dashing to her side, Harrigan knelt down and removed the gag from her mouth. Looking at the handcuffs, he asked, "Did he have the keys on him?"

"No!" she gasped. "He told me he didn't have them!"

Thinking fast, Harrigan said, "I'll have to see if I can lift the stove enough so you can pull your hands free." Then, looking up the length of stovepipe, he realized that the pipe was fitted too snugly, meaning it would have to be removed in order to lift the stove—and there were neither tools nor time to do so.

Bending down, he put his face directly in front of Ginny's in order to be heard over the roaring of the fast-closing flames. "I can't get you free that way!" he shouted. "I'll have to break the handcuffs somehow." Quickly looking around, he asked, "Is there an ax somewhere?"

Nodding, Ginny gestured toward the back, saying, "Yes, in the woodshed."

Harrigan crossed the room in two strides, went out to the shed and pulled open the door, and immediately spotted the ax. Grabbing it, he raced back inside. With sweat pouring down his face, his heart pounding in his ears, he steadied himself, taking careful aim.

Ginny reflexively closed her eyes as the sharp blade whizzed in front of her face. The blade landed precisely where Harrigan intended it to, and the links smashed apart.

Ginny rose unsteadily to her feet, and when Harrigan tried to help her, she snapped, "Let go of me! I'll take care of myself!"

The preacher realized that she had no idea just how close the flames were, and he did not want to take the time to argue with her. His jaw clenched in frustration, he protested, "You've been lied to, Ginny, but there isn't time to try to convince you right now! We've got to get out of here!"

Ginny's fury showed on her face. "I'll never believe you!" she screamed, and, wobbling slightly, she started for the door. But her legs were stiff from being on the floor so long, and she fell.

173

Harrigan scooped her up in his arms and ran outside
and he was horrified when he saw that the fire had alread
eaten up most of the town and was now no more than
hundred yards away. The heat was intense and burned hi
face as he ran toward where he had left his horse. Sud
denly he halted, his heart sinking. The terrified anima
had panicked and was galloping toward the river, leavin
Harrigan and Ginny without any means of outrunning th
fire.

Chapter Sixteen

Del Harrigan's mind was spinning. He had been in many tight spots in the Civil War, and he had learned to think and react quickly. Abruptly setting Ginny down, he told her forcefully, "Wait right here! I'll be right back!"

Before she could respond, he dashed back inside the schoolhouse. He grabbed the ax, and with a single powerful blow against the floor, he struck off the ax head. Grabbing the kerchief from where it lay on the floor, he wrapped it around the ax handle and tied it securely in place. Then, racing across the room, he pulled off the chimney from the kerosene lamp and doused the makeshift torch with the flammable liquid. A box of matches sat on the shelf, and he scooped up a handful, shoving them into his pants pocket as he darted outside.

Returning to Ginny, who stood frozen with fear, he shouted, "Here, hold this!" and shoved the torch into her hands. Then he swept her into his arms and made a run for the river. When Harrigan had covered some two hundred yards, he put Ginny down, panting from exhaustion. Looking back, he watched the schoolhouse go up in flames and the framework of the new church begin to smolder.

"There's no way we can outrun the fire!" Ginny screamed, tears running down her face.

He knew she was right. The powerful wind was driving it too fast. Abruptly, he pulled out some of the matches and tried to strike them in the rushing wind, but match after match blew out.

"What are you doing?" Ginny gasped.

Raising his voice above the whine of the wind and the thunder of the fire, he shouted, "I'm going to make a firebreak!"

He took hold of her hands and cupped them together and, using them as a shield against the wind, finally got the torch lit. Kneeling down, he brushed the flaming torch against the dry brown grass in a long line, and the grass ignited instantly, the flames spreading quickly. Within seconds the grass in the area was blazing, the wind spreading it ever farther in front of them.

Throwing down the torch, he rushed back to Ginny, taking her by the hand. "We just might make it, now!" he told her hopefully.

The blaze behind them was now no more than fifty yards away, and the heat was almost unbearable. However, the dry grass ahead of them was instantly consumed by the wind-blown flames and was quickly reduced to nothing more than harmless smoking patches.

Harrigan and Ginny followed the line of fire in front of them, steadily covering ground that had already been burned. Coming to a shallow ditch that ran horizontally in front of them, the preacher stomped out the tiny flames that remained in the ditch and ordered, "Lie facedown in there! Hurry!" When she looked at him questioningly, he added, "The fire will burn out when it reaches what's already been burned, but it'll be so close that we'll need some protection from the heat!"

Ginny obeyed instantly, pressing her body flat against the still-warm ground.

Looking back one last time, Harrigan saw that the flames were nearing the edge of the charred grass. To protect Ginny further from the intense heat, he covered her body with his own. The sound was deafening and the heat was overwhelming, and it seemed to Harrigan as if someone had opened the door of a gigantic blast furnace. The heat on his back was so intense that he wondered if his shirt would ignite.

Just when he felt he could bear the heat no longer, it dissipated. Tentatively, he lifted his head and looked around. With nothing to fuel it, the roaring inferno had cut a wide swath around them, heading for the bank of the White River. Behind them, the town of Red Buffalo was ablaze.

Harrigan lifted himself off Ginny and climbed out of the shallow ditch. Leaning down, he took hold of the schoolteacher's arms and lifted her to her feet.

Ginny was still shaking from their close brush with death, but when the preacher tried to take her in his arms to console her, she pushed him away. "Thank you for saving my life. Now I think we should go join the others across the river," she said coolly.

"Ginny, I know what you're thinking," Harrigan began, but she cut him off by turning away and heading for the riverbank. Eager to convince her of his innocence in the Helen Coffman matter, the preacher caught up to her and took her by the shoulders, telling her softly, "Saving your life was my pleasure, Ginny. I love you, and I—"

She whirled around, and the fire in her eyes burned as intensely as the prairie fire had. "There are witnesses, Del!" she spat angrily.

"What they think they saw never happened," he explained defensively.

Pulling from his grasp, Ginny wheeled and hurried toward the river, saying over her shoulder, "I don't want to talk about it. We have nothing more to say to each other—ever."

Had it not been for the pain she had suffered because of Mack's infidelities, Harrigan would have gotten angry in return at her lack of faith in him. But resigned to her anger for the moment, he merely sighed and headed toward the river behind her. When the two survivors reached the bank, the preacher took Ginny's elbow—despite her protests—and assisted her down the steep slope to the riverbed.

Standing in the shallows at the water's edge, Harrigan suggested, "Why don't you let me carry you across?"

Ginny looked down at her long skirt. "Well, I guess it

would be rather difficult in this," she muttered. "All right,'
she finally replied, her voice toneless.

Frank Meeker was the first to approach them when
they reached the other side. "Oh, Ginny!" he exclaimed.
"I'm so glad you're safe!"

Del Harrigan put Ginny Wheeler down, and the townspeople all gathered around them, their restraint evident as
they thanked the preacher for his ingenuity in saving their
beloved schoolteacher. Harrigan's heart was stricken as he
realized from their attitude that apparently every single
person in Red Buffalo had heard the story of Helen Coffman
sleeping in his room . . . and apparently every single
person believed it to be true. Losing all hope of ever
being able to convince Ginny of his innocence, he started
walking away.

"Wait a minute, Reverend!" a youthful voice called.
"I've got somethin' to say, and I want everybody to hear
it!"

Wearily looking back over his shoulder, Harrigan saw
Jimmy Boyd, the young hostler, standing defiantly with
his hands on his hips. "Jimmy, I'm too exhausted to listen
to any more angry words. Please, just let me go off by
myself."

The hostler ran up to Harrigan, grabbing hold of his
arm. "No, you don't understand." Boyd cleared his throat,
gazed around at the crowd, and told him, "Like everyone
else, Pastor Harrigan, I heard the story that Bernie Walker
and Frank Meeker have been spreadin' around town."

Glancing over at the clerk and the marshal, Harrigan
found that neither man would meet his eyes.

The hostler continued, "The story the Coffman woman
told Bernie and Frank when she came down the stairs at
the hotel around five o'clock was that she had been in your
room with you all night. She said she was slipping out
quietly because she didn't want to awaken you. Well,
when that story reached my ears, Pastor, I knew somethin'
was wrong. Actually, I knew right away that she was lyin'
through her teeth."

Harrigan stared at Jimmy Boyd, his heart pounding. Licking his dry lips, he asked, "How?"

The youth smiled. "Simple. I knew she was lyin' because I'm a light sleeper, and I heard somethin' disturbin' the horses in my corral last night. And bein' a conscientious person, I got up and looked out the window to see what was wrong. What I saw was you leadin' your horse and one of my bays through the corral gate, and I figured you were gettin' an early start for the Sioux village. I knew you were goin' to take Lone Fox's body home, so I understood why you were takin' the bay." Jimmy stared pointedly at every face in the crowd before he added, "Before I laid back down, I struck a match to read the clock. It was just past two."

A startled murmur rose from the crowd. Harrigan looked over at Ginny, who was standing just a few feet away, and saw the shocked expression on her face.

"Well, when I heard Bernie and Frank's story," proceeded Boyd, "I figured that if the Coffman woman would lie about stayin' all night in the preacher's hotel room with him, she lied about the whole thing."

Frank Meeker stepped forward, shaking his head in protest. "Wait a minute, Jimmy. If she was lying, then where'd she stay all night? Both me and Bernie saw her go upstairs, and Bernie was behind the desk all night and she didn't come back down." He looked over at the clerk. "Right?"

Walker had a sheepish expression on his face. "Well, actually I *did* fall asleep for a little while—which I guess is when the reverend left." Suddenly his head came up and his mouth dropped open. "Wait a minute!" he exclaimed. "There was a vacant room at the end of the hallway! I guess somehow Miss Coffman got into that room and stayed there!" Walker's face reddened with anger. "Why, that scheming hussy! Imagine the nerve of her—using me to work her evil deeds."

Harrigan nodded. "That makes sense. She came to my door when I was about to retire, and I immediately sent her away. That was the last I saw of her—and I have absolutely no idea where she went from there."

Stepping meekly up to Harrigan, the marshal held out his hand and said, "I'm sorry, Pastor. I hope you'll accept my apologies." He looked away from the preacher's sharp gaze, adding, "I guess I, uh, let my feelings for Ginny hide what should have been obvious—that you're a man of God who wouldn't behave that way. That was the key, wasn't it? I was a fool, Pastor, for being so quick to believe Helen Coffman and condemn you."

Harrigan accepted the apology with good grace. Then, smiling, he suggested, "Actually, there's another key that's necessary—only this one's a *real* key." He gestured toward Ginny and explained to Meeker, "You're the only one who can get those rather unattractive bracelets off Ginny's wrists."

"But how—?"

"One of Perry Prince's men kidnapped her, and he shackled her to the stove with that stolen pair of handcuffs."

The marshal's face paled. "Oh, my God," he whispered harshly. "I forgot all about them!" He looked at Harrigan with a stricken expression on his face. "I didn't get Perry Prince and his men out of the jail! I got knocked unconscious while crossing the street and Sam Johnson picked me up and put me in his wagon. I woke up on this side of the river, and by then everything was so chaotic that I didn't even remember . . ."

Harrigan sighed and rested a comforting hand on Meeker's shoulder. "I'm sorry they had to die that way, but if they hadn't been trying to harm Ginny, they wouldn't have been in the jail." He paused and then reminded the marshal, "How about giving me that key so I can free Ginny from those cuffs?"

"Oh! Sure thing."

Harrigan walked over to the woman he loved and stood in front of her. She was silently weeping with her face buried in her hands. Touching her shoulder tenderly, he said softly, "Ginny . . ."

She slowly lifted her head, looking at him through

listening eyes. Her voice quivering, she asked, "How can you even stand the sight of me?"

Stepping closer, he responded, "You mean because you doubted me?"

"Yes."

"I told you I understood why. Those scars of yours an very deep."

Ginny flung her arms around his waist. "Oh, Del!" ae sobbed. "Please forgive me! I should have known you ould never— I . . . I . . . oh, please forgive me!"

Hugging her tightly, the handsome preacher kissed er hair and whispered, "You're forgiven, darling. Let's ury it all right here and forget it."

"I'll never doubt you again," she promised, "never!"

Harrigan kissed her tenderly and then said lightly, Good. I guess that means you're still going to marry me."

Smiling through her tears, she answered, "I am, deed!"

Harrigan laughed at the forcefulness of her reply and as about to speak when a man in the crowd approached im and said, "By the way, Reverend, I don't think anyody's yet said how much we appreciate your going to the ioux village. I think I can speak for everyone when I say e'd all like to hear what happened."

Climbing up onto a wagon bed, Harrigan announced the worried citizens of Red Buffalo that there would be o more trouble from Eagle Claw. A great cheer went up om the crowd, and when it died down, he told them how e had convinced the chief that the people of the town aeant no harm to his people, and that the murder of the ld Sioux was an isolated incident involving three bigoted aen.

With the Sioux threat off their minds, the people of ed Buffalo began talking about what they were going to o. It took only a few minutes before there was unanimous greement that they would rebuild their town.

"If I may make a suggestion," Del Harrigan offered, it might be better if we give it a new name." Scratching

his head, he added with a grin, "Perhaps naming a tow
after a prairie fire wasn't the best thing to do."

Everyone laughingly agreed. They would come u
with a new name while they were rebuilding—and th
time they would encircle the town with a wide grassle
band.

Another rousing cheer swept through the crowd, whic
soon broke up to gather around individual wagons. D
Harrigan looked around for Ginny, and he caught sight
her standing at the river's edge, apart from the other
She was staring off toward the ruins of the town lit now b
the breaking dawn.

Going to her, Harrigan folded her in his arms an
softly asked, "Tell me, darling, when would you like to g
married?"

Before Ginny could answer, someone shouted, "Indian
Every eye was turned to see a large band of Sioux led b
Chief Eagle Claw riding slowly toward them along th
riverbank. Harrigan could make out several heavily lade
wagons at the rear of the column, and as the chief dre
abreast, Eagle Claw raised a hand and the column of Siou
warriors halted.

Sliding from his horse's back, the venerable chi
shook hands Indian-style with the preacher. Then, speak
ing loudly, he explained, "We observed the fire of the re
buffalo from our village, and we knew it would destro
your town. We wish you to know that Eagle Claw and h
people are your friends. We bring food and tepees an
wish to help you build your town again."

The people were jubilant. In their exhilaration, the
hugged not only each other, they also hugged the Indian
who at first looked startled and then laughed.

Suddenly Ginny Wheeler called for quiet, and raisin
her voice so that everyone could hear, she declared, '
just want you all to understand that we're going to have t
get another preacher in our new town."

The crowd immediately fell silent and everyone, in
cluding Harrigan, looked at her aghast. Ginny then eye
her man lovingly and added with a smile, "Reveren

Delbert Wade Harrigan, you are a man of many talents and abilities, but there is one thing you cannot do."

Swallowing hard, Harrigan asked, "What's that?"

Broadening her smile, Ginny replied sweetly, "Perform your own wedding ceremony!"

★ WAGONS WEST ★

A series of unforgettable books that trace the lives of a dauntless band of pioneering men, women, and children as they brave the hazards of an untamed land in their trek across America. This legendary caravan of people forge a new link in the wilderness. They are Americans from the North and the South, alongside immigrants, Blacks, and Indians, who wage fierce daily battles for survival on this uncompromising journey—each to their private destinies as they fulfill their greatest dreams.

Special Offer
Buy a Bantam Book
for only 50¢.

Now you can have Bantam's catalog filled with hundreds of titles plus take advantage of our unique and exciting bonus book offer. A special offer which gives you the opportunity to purchase a Bantam book for only 50¢. Here's how!

By ordering any five books at the regular price per order, you can also choose any other single book listed (up to a $5.95 value) for just 50¢. Some restrictions do apply, but for further details why not send for Bantam's catalog of titles today!

Just send us your name and address and we will send you a catalog!